Dread Mountain

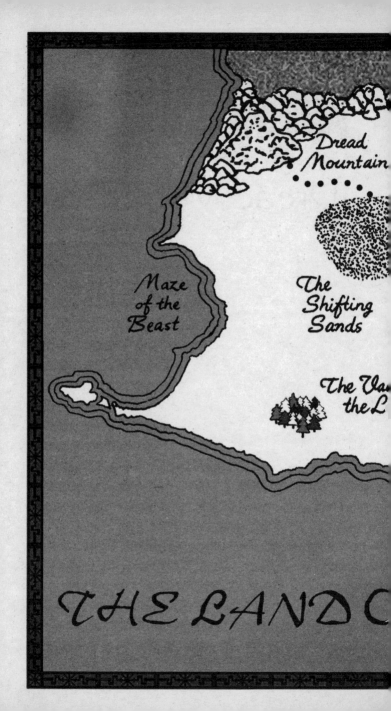

Dread
Mountain

Maze
of the
Beast

The
Shifting
Sands

The Va
the L

THE LAND O

The Shadowlands

The Lake
of Tears

The Forests
of Silence

Del

DELTORA

N
W — E
S

VENTURE INTO DELTORA

DELTORA QUEST

Dread Mountain

EMILY RODDA

Scholastic Inc.

New York Toronto London Auckland Sydney
Mexico City New Delhi Hong Kong Buenos Aires

No part of this publication may be reproduced in whole or in part, or stored in a retrieval system, or transmitted in any form or by any means, electronic, mechanical, photocopying, recording, or otherwise, without written permission of the publisher. For information regarding permission, write to Scholastic Australia, PO Box 579, Lindfield, New South Wales, Australia 2070.

ISBN 0-439-25327-6

24 23 **22 21 20** 19 18 17 16 15 14 13   7/0

Printed in the U.S.A.   40

First Scholastic club printing, August 2001

Contents

The story so far . . .

Sixteen-year-old Lief, fulfilling a pledge made by his father before he was born, is on a great quest to find the seven gems of the magic Belt of Deltora. The gems — an amethyst, a topaz, a diamond, a ruby, an opal, a lapis lazuli, and an emerald — were stolen to open the way for the evil Shadow Lord to invade Deltora. Hidden in fearsome places throughout the land, they must be restored to the Belt before the heir to the throne can be found and the Shadow Lord's tyranny ended.

Lief's companions are the man Barda, who was once a Palace guard, and Jasmine, a girl of Lief's own age who they met in the fearful Forests of Silence.

On their travels they have discovered a secret resistance movement led by Doom, a mysterious scar-faced man who rescued them when they were captured by the Shadow Lord's brutal Grey Guards.

So far the companions have found four gems. The golden topaz, symbol of faith, has the power to contact the spirit world and to clear the mind. The ruby, symbol of happiness, pales when danger threatens, repels evil spirits, and is an antidote to venom. The opal, gem of hope, gives glimpses of the future. The lapis lazuli, the heavenly stone, is a powerful talisman.

To find the fifth stone, they must travel almost to the border of the Shadowlands itself. To the fabled Dread Mountain.

Now read on . . .

1 ~ Refuge

The day had been fine and clear and there was a slight chill in the air. It was perfect weather for walking, but nothing is pleasant when you are thirsty, tired, and afraid. Lief trudged along, his head bowed, his limbs aching, only dimly aware of Barda and Jasmine moving beside him.

The water bottles were almost empty. Ever since leaving the Shifting Sands the companions had been existing on a few mouthfuls of water a day. But still the flat brown countryside stretched away from them with no sign of river or stream, and the sky, flooded now with the orange of the setting sun, was huge and cloudless.

Lief was walking with his head bent so he would not have to look at the ragged horizon. Dread Mountain was still far distant. It would be weeks before the companions reached it — if they did not die of thirst first, Lief thought grimly — but the very thought of it filled him with fear. The knowledge that every step he took brought him closer to the Shadowlands border was more terrifying still.

He hunched his shoulders, thinking with wonder of the boy who had left Del so filled with excitement at the thought of the adventure ahead. That boy now seemed absurdly young. And that time seemed very long ago.

Yet it was not so long — just a few months — and much had been achieved in that time. Four gems now glowed in the Belt of Deltora hidden under Lief's shirt. There were only three stones left to find. Lief knew he should feel happy, hopeful, and triumphant, as Jasmine did. Instead, he was battling gloom and despair.

For, as he looked back, it seemed miraculous to him that the gems had been secured at all. It seemed miraculous that he and his companions had survived the terrors they had faced. For how much longer could such good luck last? Lief's spirit shrank at the thought of what was ahead.

So far too they had escaped the attention of the Shadow Lord, but this time had surely ended. Doom, the scar-faced leader of the Resistance, had said that word was spreading about them. And if Doom had heard whispers, the Shadow Lord had certainly heard them too. Yet here Lief, Barda, and Jasmine walked, in the open air, under the open sky, with Kree flying ahead of them. What did it matter that no one knew their names? The description was enough.

Lief jumped nervously and nearly stumbled as a black shape flapped beside his head. But it was only Kree, landing on Jasmine's arm. The bird screeched. Filli poked his furry grey head out of Jasmine's jacket and chattered excitedly.

"Kree says there is water ahead," Jasmine cried. "A small pool — a spring, perhaps, for he could see no stream leading to it. It is in a grove of trees not far from the road."

The thought of water made them all quicken their pace, and it was not long before Kree took flight again and led them off the road. Dodging bushes and rocks, they followed him until at last they entered a grove of pale, odd-looking trees.

And there, sure enough, right in the center, was a small round pool surrounded by white stones. Eagerly they ran towards it. Then they saw that fixed to one of the stones was a dull brass plate with words engraved upon it — words they could just make out in the dimming light:

DREAMING SPRING

DRINK, GENTLE STRANGER,
AND WELCOME.

ALL OF EVIL WILL BEWARE.

The companions hesitated. The spring was clear and tempting. Their thirst was very great. But the words on the brass plate made them all nervous. Was the water safe to drink?

"Jasmine, what do the trees say?" muttered Barda. Once Barda had doubted Jasmine's ability to talk to growing things, but this time had long passed.

Jasmine frowned. "They do not say anything," she said, looking around. "They are completely silent. I do not understand it."

Lief shivered. The grove was green and still. Lush, soft grass grew underfoot. It was like a little paradise, yet there was a strange feeling in the air. He ran his tongue over his dry lips. "It might be better if we do not drink from this spring," he said reluctantly. "It could be enchanted — or poisoned."

"We are not of evil will," Barda protested. "Surely it will be safe for us."

But he remained where he was, and did not approach the spring.

Filli chattered impatiently on Jasmine's shoulder.

"We are all thirsty, Filli," Jasmine murmured. "But we must wait. We are not sure — Filli! No!"

The little creature had leaped to the ground. He scuttled to the pool, ignoring Jasmine's cries. In a moment he had dipped his head into the crystal waters and was drinking deeply.

"Filli!" called Jasmine in despair.

But for once Filli was not listening. He was lost

in the joy of quenching his terrible thirst.

And he did not become sick. He did not fall.

Kree was the next to fly to the spring. He, too, drank, dipping his beak and tipping back his head over and over again. He too showed no ill effects. And after that, Lief, Barda, and Jasmine could wait no longer, but ran to the pool themselves.

The water was cold and sweet. Never had Lief tasted anything so good. At home in Del the water was just as cold, but always tasted of the metal pump.

When at last they had drunk as much as they needed, the companions filled their water bottles to the brim in case they had to make a quick escape in the night. The grove seemed safe, but they had learned that it was unwise to trust appearances.

They sat on the grass and ate as the moon rose and stars appeared in the sky above them. It was cold, but they had decided against making a fire. Even a small blaze would be like a beacon, signalling their presence. Also for safety's sake, they moved well into the cover of the trees before unrolling their blankets. Others might know of the spring and come to drink from it in the night.

"How careful we have become," yawned Jasmine, gathering her blanket around her. "I remember a time when we were bolder."

"Things are different now," muttered Lief. "Now they are looking for us." He shivered.

Barda glanced at him quickly, then turned away

5

to mask the concern in his eyes. "We will sleep in turns. I will take the first watch," he said.

Kree squawked.

"You need sleep too, Kree," smiled Jasmine. "You are very tired. You cannot guard us all night long. You and Filli and I will watch together when Barda wakes us."

She turned over and closed her eyes, her hand in Filli's soft fur. Drowsily Lief watched as Kree began to flutter up to a tree branch above her head. Then the bird seemed to change his mind, wheeling and dropping back down to the grass. He hopped close to Jasmine and settled there, tucking his head under his wing.

Lief felt a small flicker of fear. "Barda," he called softly. "Look at Kree."

Barda, hunched beneath the blanket he had thrown around himself for warmth, stirred and turned around.

"Why is he sleeping on the ground instead of perching on a branch?" Lief whispered.

"Perhaps he does not like the trees," Barda whispered back. "Jasmine said they were silent. And certainly they are strange. Have you noticed that they look exactly alike?"

Lief looked around him and realized that Barda was right. That was one of the reasons why the trees looked so odd. Every single one had the same straight, smooth trunk, the same three branches pointing to the sky, the same thick clusters of pale leaves. His spine tingled.

"Lief, stop worrying, I beg you!" Barda growled after a moment. "Whatever is troubling Kree, it is not enough to stop him from taking his rest. I suggest you follow his example. You will regret it if you do not. Your turn to keep watch will come soon enough."

Slowly Lief pulled his blanket more tightly around him and lay down. For a minute or two he stared up at the star-spangled night sky framed by the pale leaves of the strange trees. Not a breath of wind stirred the leaves. No insects chirped. There was no sound at all except for Jasmine's soft breathing.

His eyelids grew heavy. Soon he could not keep them open, and he did not try. If Kree is not afraid to sleep, neither am I, he thought. After all, what can befall us while Barda is keeping watch?

In moments he was asleep. So he did not see Barda's head droop gently to his chest. He did not hear Barda's quiet snores.

And he did not feel the passing of silent feet as the dwellers of the grove moved softly to the Dreaming Spring.

2 - Before Dawn

Lief was dreaming. The dream seemed very real. He was standing by the old pump in the forge yard. The yard was dark and deserted. It is night, he thought. Mother and Father will be inside at this hour. But the house was dark too, and though he called from the door, and again from the kitchen, no one answered.

Confused, but not yet frightened, he walked into the living room. Light from the full moon shone through the window. The curtains had not been drawn. That was odd. And things were lying on the floor: books and papers, scattered everywhere. His parents would never have left them that way.

Their bedroom was empty, the bed tumbled and unmade, clothing lying on the floor. There was a jar of dead flowers on the chest. Now he knew that something was wrong. In fear, he ran outside once more.

The moon shone down on the empty yard. The forge gate was swinging. There was a mark on it. He could not quite see what it was. He moved closer, his heart thudding. Then he saw it.

Lief woke with a start. Sweat was beading his forehead, he was breathing fast, and his hands were trembling. He told himself that he had been dreaming, dreaming. There was nothing to fear.

Slowly he realized that the sky above him was pale and the stars had almost disappeared. It was nearly dawn. He had slept the night through. But — surely Jasmine, who had taken the second watch, had not forgotten to call him?

He glanced over to where he had seen Jasmine settling to rest the night before. She was still lying there, breathing quietly and evenly. Kree was huddled beside her. And not far away sat Barda, his back against a tree, his head on his chest. He too was sleeping soundly.

Lief almost laughed. So, despite their sensible

plans, they had all slept. Perhaps it was as well. They needed rest, and as it happened, nothing had troubled them in the night.

He felt very thirsty. Silently he unrolled himself from his blanket, got up, and moved through the trees towards the spring. His bare feet made no noise at all on the soft grass. That was something else about the grove that was unusual, he realized — the trees seemed to shed no leaves or sticks at all.

He had almost reached the spring when he heard it: a soft splashing sound. Someone — or something — was drinking.

Lief's hand crept to the hilt of his sword. He half-turned, thinking to wake Barda and Jasmine. But he was so near to the spring now that it seemed foolish not to at least peep at whatever had entered the grove. Holding his breath, he stole around the last tree and looked.

A plump shape was bent over the water, lapping. It was an animal of some kind — about as big as a large dog, but far rounder than any dog Lief had ever seen. Lief narrowed his eyes, struggling to see it clearly in the dim light. The creature was a rich, chestnut brown. It seemed to have no fur, and its ears were small and set close to its head. It had short, stubby back legs, and slender front paws. The skin on its back and sides was oddly marked, folded, and rippled.

What was it?

He took a step forward, and at the same moment

the creature straightened, turned, and saw him.

Lief gazed at wide, startled dark eyes, whiskers stiff with fright, a pink, open mouth, and small front paws clasped together in fear, and the strangest feeling of pleasure and peace flowed through him. He could not understand it, but he knew one thing clearly: the creature was harmless, gentle, and very frightened.

"Do not be afraid," he said in a low, soothing voice. "I will not harm you."

The creature still stared at him. But Lief thought that some of the fear had left its eyes, to be replaced by curiosity.

"I will not harm you," he repeated. "I am a friend."

"What is your name?" the creature asked in a squeaky voice.

Lief jumped violently. It had not occurred to him that it could speak. "My name is Lief," he said, without thinking.

"I am Little — I mean, Prin, daughter of the Kin," said the creature. She stood upright and began waddling towards Lief, her short legs toiling across the grass, her front paws bent, her mouth curved into a sweet and hopeful smile.

Lief's jaw dropped in astonishment. Waves of memory were flooding over him. No wonder he had felt that feeling of peace when first he saw Prin's face. How could he not have realized before what she was?

Kin! The fabled flying creatures that every child in Del knew of. Had Lief not had a toy Kin, Monty, to sleep with from his earliest days? His mother had made Monty out of soft brown fabric stuffed with straw, and over the years the little creature had grown worn and battered. Now he was kept hidden away in a drawer with other treasures, well out of sight of teasing friends. But once he had been Lief's trusted companion and comforter, carried around everywhere. How often in those days had Lief wished that Monty would come to life?

And this creature could be that wish come true, Lief thought. It could be Monty walking towards him over the grass. But surely — surely he had been told that the gentle, kindly Kin died out long ago? Surely they only existed now in old tales and picture books?

Lief swallowed, and for a moment wondered if he was still dreaming. But Prin was standing in front of him, large as life. Now he could see that she did have fur after all — a silken fuzz like fine brown moss. Her folded wings were covered with the same velvety stuff. He longed to stroke them, to see if they were as soft as they looked.

"Will you play with me, Lief?" asked Prin, twitching her whiskers and bouncing up and down on her toes. "Will you play hide-and-find?"

Lief realized then that she was very young. And of course she must be! Standing upright she only reached his shoulder. But fully grown Kin, he had been told, were so large that people in the old days, looking up and seeing them in the sky, had sometimes taken them for dragons and tried to shoot them down.

"Where is your family?" he asked, looking around. "Should you not ask — ?"

"They are still dreaming!" said Prin scornfully. "They will not wake till long after the sun comes up. See?"

She pointed to what Lief had taken to be groups of huge rocks scattered among and beyond the trees. To his amazement, Lief saw that they were not rocks at all, but Kin, curled up so tightly that all that could be seen of them were their hunched backs.

"I am supposed to stay curled until they wake," said Prin, lowering her voice. "But it is not fair. I have nothing interesting to dream of. I would rather play. Now — you hide and I will sing. I will not cheat, I promise! I will sing slowly, and I will close my ears as well as my eyes. Ready? Go!"

She put her paws over her eyes and began to sing.

"You can hide but I will find you,
My sharp eyes will seek you out . . ."

Lief quickly realized that the song was used by Kin children instead of counting. At the end of her song Prin would open her eyes and expect to find him gone. Not wishing to disappoint her, he ran away quickly and hid behind one of the trees in the thickest part of the grove.

It was not a very clever hiding place, but he did not want to stray far from where Jasmine and Barda were sleeping, and at least it would show the little Kin that he wanted to be friendly.

Flattening himself against the trunk of the tree, he smiled to himself as he listened to her voice squeaking on towards the end of the song.

". . . You can hide but I will find you,

Flap your wings and you'll be out!

You can hide but I will find you.

My sharp eyes will — oh!"

With a choking squeak the song broke off. There was a burst of loud, harsh laughter.

"Got it!" roared a voice. "Yo, help me! It's putting up a fight."

Horrified, Lief crept out from behind his tree and peered back to the spring. Two Grey Guards were bending over a struggling bundle on the ground. The bundle was Prin.

They had thrown a jacket over her head, and now were winding her round and around with rope.

"Give it a kick, Carn 4," the second Guard growled. "That'll teach it."

Lief smothered a cry as Carn 4 kicked savagely and the bundle stilled.

3 - Evil Will

L ief took a step forward, then jumped as a hand gripped his arm. It was Barda, his eyes swollen with sleep. Jasmine was right behind him.

"Come away, Lief," Barda whispered under his breath. "They are going to rest and eat. We can be long gone by the time they are ready to leave."

Lief shook his head violently, his eyes still fixed on the figures by the spring. "I cannot go," he hissed. "I cannot let them kill my friend."

He saw Barda and Jasmine exchange glances and knew that they must think he had lost his wits. "There is no time to explain. Where are the blisters?" he breathed. "Go and get them."

Without a word Jasmine slipped away into the trees. She might think Lief was being foolish, but she was not going to let him face the Guards with only a sword to protect himself.

With Barda close behind him, Lief began moving closer to the spring, running from tree to tree until he was very near to where Prin was lying.

"Pig for breakfast," Carn 4 was crowing. "Nothing better."

"It's not a pig," the other one said. "Look at its feet."

"It's fat, whatever it is. It'll be good eating." Carn 4 straightened his back and went over to the spring, taking the cap off his water bottle.

"We smelled out this water just in time, Carn 5," he called, tipping up the bottle and shaking it to show how empty it was.

Lief heard Barda draw a sharp breath. "They are members of the Carn pod," Barda breathed. "Like . . ."

"I know," Lief whispered in reply. "Like the Guards who caught us in Rithmere."

His hand was slippery on the hilt of his sword. Did Carn 4 and 5 know or guess what had happened to their brothers in the Shifting Sands? Had they taken over where Carn 2 and Carn 8 had left off, to save their pod from disgrace?

Carn 5 strolled over to join his fellow at the spring, rubbing his nose with the back of his hand. "This place stinks of ticks," he complained.

Lief held his breath.

"Not ours, though." Carn 4 bent to fill his bottle. "Our two and their friend went straight on. That big

16

ugly one — the one they call Glock — he drags his feet. You can smell every step he takes. He didn't come in here."

Lief's heart was thudding wildly. So Doom had released Glock and Neridah, as he had planned. Carn 4 and 5 must have been Glock and Neridah's captors. Now they were pursuing them just as Carn 2 and Carn 8 had pursued Lief and his companions after their escape.

The Guards were both facing the spring. Now was the time to try to get Prin away. Lief glanced urgently over his shoulder. Where was Jasmine with the blisters?

"We'll get them by nightfall," Carn 5 said confidently, kneeling down beside Carn 4 and plunging his own water bottle into the water. "Them and whoever let them go. And won't we make *him* sorry for himself?"

"We'll have some fun with him," the other agreed.

They both laughed and bent to drink, sucking and lapping noisily.

Lief knew he could not wait. He could not miss his chance. Ignoring Barda's restraining hand on his arm, he darted into the open, seized the limp bundle that was Prin, and began dragging it away.

Afterwards, he cursed himself for his stupid thoughtlessness. He had just assumed that Prin was unconscious. But Prin was very much awake, lying motionless in an agony of fear. Feeling unknown hands upon her she squealed in terror.

Instantly the Guards leaped to their feet and whirled around, still swallowing the water in their mouths, their blisters and slings already in their dripping hands. They saw Lief bent over Prin. Snarling, they rushed towards them.

"Lief! Run!" Lief heard Barda roar, as the big man lunged forward trying to push him out of the way. But Lief was frozen to the spot. He was gaping in shock.

For the Guards were screaming. They were staggering, stopping. Their feet were sprouting roots that snaked into the earth, tying them in place. Their legs were drawing together, hardening into a solid trunk. Their bodies, arms, and necks were stretching towards the sky, and pale leaves were forcing their way through skin that was becoming smooth bark.

And in moments, two trees stood in their places. Two new trees for the grove — as silent, still, and perfect as all the others.

Jasmine came running, with Filli chattering in fear on her shoulder. "The rocks are coming alive!" she panted. "They are coming this way!"

✳

Half an hour later, still dazed, Lief, Barda, and Jasmine were sitting among a group of huge Kin. Filli was staring, wide-eyed, at the great creatures. Prin, complaining bitterly, had been made to climb into her mother's pouch.

"You must stay curled until we awake, Little One!" her mother scolded. "How many times have I told you? Now see what has happened. Those evil ones might have killed you!"

"They drank the water, Mother," sulked Prin from the depths of the pouch. "I knew they would."

"You could not know that they would drink before they did you harm!" her mother snapped. "Be still. Your side is badly bruised."

"We drank the water also!" exclaimed Barda, who was gazing from the Kin to the motionless trees in pure amazement.

Prin poked her head out of the pouch and twitched her whiskers. "Those who mean no harm can drink without harm," she chanted, plainly repeating something she had been taught.

Her mother ignored her and turned to Barda. "We knew you were of good heart when you drank from the spring and remained unharmed," she said in her slow, deep voice. "Sure that you were not a danger to us, we dreamed peacefully last night — little knowing that our child would be a danger to you in the morning. We are sorry."

Barda bowed. "It was my friend who helped the little one," he said, gesturing to Lief. "But for my part, it is a privilege to meet you. I never thought to see the Kin in my lifetime."

"We are few now," said an old Kin standing beside Prin's mother. "Since we left our Mountain — "

"Dread Mountain! You lived on Dread Mountain once, did you not? Why did you leave?" Lief interrupted, able to keep silent no longer.

The old Kin stopped, and looked at Barda.

Barda smiled. "As you see, I too have young ones in my care," he said, to Lief's annoyance. "Please forgive the interruption and continue."

"The gnomes of Dread Mountain had always tried to hunt us," said the old one. "But their arrows could not do us great harm. Our main dangers were Grey Guards and Vraal beasts, coming from the Shadowlands. But long ago something changed . . ."

His voice trailed off and he bent his head.

"The gnomes began using poison on their arrow tips," said Prin's mother, taking up the story. "It was deadly poison, and killed painfully and quickly. Many of us died." Her voice sank to a whisper. "It was a terrible time. I was very young then. But I remember."

The other Kin nodded and whispered among themselves. Plainly they too remembered.

"At last, the few of us that were left decided we could stay on the Mountain no longer," the old Kin rumbled. "This grove used to be our winter home — a good place for the growing young. Now we are here all year long. Now we can visit our Mountain — see the Boolong trees, hear the rippling streams, and smell the sweet, cool air — only in our dreams."

A feeling of sadness swept over the group. There was a long silence. Jasmine fidgeted uncomfortably.

"I had a strange dream last night," she said, plainly trying to bring a little cheer to the gathering. "I dreamed I saw the man Doom. He was in a cave full of people. The boy Dain was there — and Neridah, and Glock, and many others. Glock was eating soup, spilling it all down his chin. I called to them, but they did not hear me. It was so real!"

The old Kin looked at her. "Do you not understand? It *was* real," he said. He waved a paw at the spring. "This is the Dreaming Spring. Whatever or whoever you picture in your mind when you drink, you visit in spirit when you sleep."

"We ourselves visit our Mountain every night," Prin's mother added, as Jasmine looked disbelieving. "It comforts us greatly to see it as it is now. The Boolong trees grow thickly — far more thickly than they once did. Of course, we cannot eat the cones, but at least we are there, and together."

"Not me!" said Prin loudly. "I cannot go there. I have never seen it! I have never known anywhere but here. So I have nothing to dream of. It is not fair!"

Her mother bent over her, murmuring. The other adults looked at one another sadly.

"What I saw in my dream was *real*?" Jasmine gasped.

"So Doom, Neridah, and Glock have reached the Resistance stronghold in safety!" Barda exclaimed. He

21

looked with satisfaction at the two new trees by the spring. "And now no Guards will trouble them."

He grinned. "I dreamed of Manus and the Ralad people. I stood by the stream in their underground town. They were singing, and all was well. That is very good to know."

But Lief sat in silence, numb with shock. He was remembering his own dream, and slowly facing the knowledge that it too had been true.

4 - The Plan

At length, the gathering of the Kin broke up as each creature moved off to feed on the grass that grew beneath and beyond the trees.

"Grass is all we have here," Prin's mother explained to Lief, Barda, and Jasmine as she toiled away with her heavy young one in her pouch. "It is nourishing enough, but we have grown tired of its sweetness and long for the leaves and cones of the Boolong trees. The leaves of the trees in this grove are not fit to eat. They are not truly alive."

Kree, perched on Jasmine's arm, squawked in disgust. "Kree always knew the trees were not as they should be," Jasmine said, shuddering as she looked around her. "No wonder they are silent. It is horrible to think of them standing here, unchanging, for centuries."

"And it is fortunate for us that we passed the

23

spring's test," said Barda grimly. "Or we would be with them."

Lief had not spoken for a long time. When the last of the Kin had departed Jasmine turned to him.

"What is the matter?" she demanded. "All is well."

"All is not well," Lief muttered. "My mother and father — " He broke off, swallowing desperately to hold back tears.

"Jarred and Anna?" Barda exclaimed, looking alert. "What do you . . . ?" Suddenly his face changed, filling with fear as he understood. "You had a dream!" he exclaimed. "Lief — "

Lief nodded slowly. "The forge is empty," he said in a low voice. "The Shadow Lord's brand is on the gate. I think — I think they are dead."

Stricken with shock and grief, Barda stared at him wildly. Then his mouth firmed. "Very likely they are not dead, but simply taken prisoner," he said. "We must not give up hope."

"To be a prisoner of the Shadow Lord is worse than death," Lief whispered. "Father told me that, many times. He was always warning me . . ." The words choked in his throat and he covered his face with his hands.

Awkwardly, Jasmine put her arm around him and Filli jumped onto his shoulder, brushing his cheek with soft fur. Kree clucked sorrowfully. But Barda stood apart, struggling with his own fear and sorrow.

Finally Lief looked up. His face was very pale. "I must go back," he said.

Barda shook his head. "You must not."

"I must!" Lief insisted angrily. "How can I go on, knowing what I know?"

"You know nothing but that the forge is empty," Barda said evenly. "Jarred and Anna could be in the dungeons of the palace in Del. They could be in the Shadowlands. They could be in hiding. Or, as you said before, they could be dead. Wherever they are, you cannot help them. Your duty is here."

"Do not speak to me of duty!" Lief shouted. "They are my parents!"

"They are my friends," Barda said, still in that same expressionless voice. "My dear and only friends, Lief, since before you were born. I know what they would say to you if they could. They would tell you that our quest is their quest too. They would beg you not to abandon it."

Lief's anger died, leaving dull sadness in its place. He searched Barda's face and saw the pain behind the grim mask.

"You are right," he mumbled. "I am sorry."

Barda put a hand on his shoulder. "One thing is clear," he said. "Time has become of the first importance. We must reach Dread Mountain with all speed."

"I cannot see that we can move any faster than we have been doing," Jasmine put in.

"On foot we cannot," Barda agreed. "But I have a plan." His face was shadowed with grief, but still he managed a small smile. "Why should the Kin dream of home, instead of seeing it with their own eyes? Why should we walk, when we can fly?"

✳

Barda talked to the Kin for a very long time. He argued well. But it was not until sunset that three of them finally agreed to carry the companions to Dread Mountain.

The three who agreed were Merin, Ailsa, and Bruna. They were among the largest in the group, and all were female, for only the female Kin had pouches in which to carry passengers.

All three agreed for different reasons: Merin because she was so homesick, Ailsa because she was adventurous, and Bruna because she felt that the Kin owed Lief a debt for trying to save Prin.

"She is very dear to us all," Bruna explained. "The only young one to be born to us since we moved here from our Mountain."

"This is because we need the Mountain air and the Boolong trees to thrive," Merin cried. "Here, we just exist. On our Mountain, we can grow and breed. We should have gone back long ago."

"Gone back to die? What foolishness you talk, Merin!" snapped the old one, who had been greatly angered by the three's agreement to go. "If you, Ailsa, and Bruna go back in flesh and blood to Dread Mountain, you will surely be killed. Then there will be three less Kin, and we will have three more deaths to mourn."

"What is the use of staying here to die slowly?" snapped Ailsa, lifting her great wings. "With no babies to carry on our line, we have no future. The Kin are finished. I would rather die quickly, in a good cause, than linger here."

"We have our dreams," Prin's mother said quietly.

"I am sick of dreaming!" Ailsa exclaimed.

"And I cannot dream at all!" squeaked Prin. She ran over to Ailsa and clasped her paws. "Take me with you to the Mountain, Ailsa," she begged. "Then I too will have seen it. Then I can go with you when you dream."

Ailsa shook her head. "You cannot come, Little One. You are too precious. But think of this: you can dream of us. Then you will see where we are, and what we are doing. Will that not be just as good as travelling yourself?"

Plainly, Prin did not think so, for she began to wail and cry, paying no attention to her mother's orders and pleadings. At last her mother hurried her away, but even when they were out of sight, the sound of their arguing voices floated back through the trees. The other Kin looked distressed.

The old one frowned. "You see what you have done?" he mumbled to Barda, Lief, and Jasmine. "We were peaceful and happy here, before you came. Now there is anger between us and Little One is unhappy."

"It is not fair to blame the strangers, Crenn," Bruna objected. "Merin, Ailsa, and I have agreed to go to the Mountain of our own free will."

"That is true," said Merin gently. "And Little One is only saying what she has been saying these past few years, Crenn. The older she grows, the more she will say it. Her life here, with no companions of her own age, is too quiet for her. She is very like Ailsa — lively and adventurous."

"And she does not have dreams to lull her, as I have had," Ailsa put in. Her bright eyes turned to Jasmine, Lief, and Barda. "I think I must thank the strangers for disturbing my peace," she added. "This day has made me feel that I am alive again."

Crenn sat very upright. His old face, the whiskers white, the eyes faded and full of longing, was turned to the Mountain. The sun had dipped below the horizon when at last he spoke.

"Of course you speak the truth, all of you," he said reluctantly. "And if this must be, it must be. I only pray that you will be safe, and beg you to take care, and return to us with all speed."

"We will," Ailsa promised. She smiled around. "I will drink from the spring now, but not again this night. Then I will sleep only lightly. One of us must be awake to call the others tomorrow morning. We must leave before dawn."

5 - The Enemy

That night, Lief dreamed again. He had planned for it, drinking deeply from the spring and thinking of his father and mother while he did so. If they are dead, then it is better to face it, he told himself. If they are alive, this is my chance to find out where they are.

As he and his companions prepared for sleep, the thought of what he was about to find out made him silent and tense. He said nothing to Barda and Jasmine but perhaps they guessed what he was planning, for they were equally silent, bidding each other good night, then saying no more. Lief was grateful. This was something he had to face alone, and speaking of it would not help.

Sleep did not come quickly. For a long time he lay awake, staring up at the sky. But at last the drowsiness caused by the spring water overcame him.

This time, the dream began almost at once.

The smell was what he noticed first — the smell of damp and decay. Then there were sounds — people groaning and crying somewhere not far away, their muffled voices echoing and ghostly. It was very dark.

I am in a tomb, he thought, with a thrill of terror. But then his eyes became used to the darkness and he saw that he was in a dungeon. A figure, head bowed, was sitting on the floor in a corner.

It was his father.

Completely forgetting that he was in the cell only in spirit, Lief called out, ran over to the slumped figure, and seized its arm. His hands went straight through the solid flesh. His father remained bowed in misery, plainly hearing and feeling nothing. Hot tears springing into his eyes, Lief called again. This time, his father stirred and raised his head. He looked straight at Lief, a slight, puzzled frown on his face.

"Yes, Father, yes! It is me!" Lief cried. "Oh, try to hear me! What has happened? Where is this place? Is Mother — ?"

But his father was sighing deeply and bowing his head again. "Dreaming," he murmured to himself.

"It is not a dream!" shouted Lief. "I am here! Father — "

His father's head jerked up. A key was grating in the lock of the cell door. Lief swung around as the door creaked open. Three figures stood there — a tall,

30

thin man in long robes backed by two huge guards holding flaming torches. For a moment Lief was panic-stricken, convinced that his cries had been heard. But immediately he realized that the newcomers were as unaware of him as his father was.

"So, Jarred!" The man in the long robes took a torch from one of the guards and moved into the center of the cell. Lit by the flickering light of the flame, his face was sharp, the cheekbones deeply shadowed, the thin mouth cruel.

"Prandine!" breathed Lief's father.

Lief's heart thudded. Prandine? King Endon's chief advisor, the secret servant of the Shadow Lord? But surely he was dead? Surely —

The man smiled. "Not Prandine, blacksmith," he sneered. "The one called Prandine fell to his death from the tower of this very palace over sixteen years ago, on the day the Master claimed his kingdom. Prandine was careless — or unlucky. Perhaps you know something about that?"

"I know nothing."

"We shall see. But where one dies, there is always another to take his place. The Master likes this face and form. He chose to repeat it in me. My name is Fallow."

"Where is my wife?"

Lief caught his breath. The thin man sneered.

"Would it please you to know? Perhaps I will tell you — if you answer my questions."

"What questions? Why have we been brought here? We have done nothing wrong."

Fallow turned to the door, where the guards stood watching. "Leave us!" he ordered. "I will question the prisoner alone."

The guards nodded, and withdrew.

As soon as the door was firmly closed, the thin man took something from the folds of his robe. A small pale blue book.

It was *The Belt of Deltora*, the book Jarred had found hidden in the palace library. The book Lief himself had so often studied as he grew up, and which had taught him so much about the power of the Belt and its gems.

Lief squirmed to see it in this man's hands. He longed to snatch it away from Fallow, save his father from this cruel taunting. But he was powerless. All he could do was stand and watch.

"This book was found in your house, Jarred," Fallow was saying. "How did it come there?"

"I do not remember."

"Perhaps I can help you. It is known to us. It came from the palace library."

"As a young man I lived in the palace. I may have taken it away with me when I left. It was many years ago. I do not know."

Fallow tapped the book with bony fingers. The cruel smile never left his face.

"The Master thinks you have deceived us,

32

Jarred," he said. "He thinks you kept in contact with your foolish young friend, King Endon, and at the last helped him, his idiot bride, and their unborn brat to escape."

Lief's father shook his head. "Endon was fool enough to believe me a traitor," he said in a low, even voice. "Endon would never have turned to me for help, nor would I have given it to him."

"So we thought. But now we are not so sure. Strange things have been occurring in the kingdom, blacksmith. Things my Master does not like."

Lief saw a sudden flash of hope in his father's downturned eyes. He glanced quickly at Fallow. Had he seen it too?

He had. His own eyes were gleaming coldly as he went on.

"Certain allies, valued by the Master, have been viciously killed. Certain — goods — also valued by the Master have been stolen," Fallow went on. "We suspect that King Endon is still alive. We suspect that he is making some last, useless effort to reclaim his kingdom. What do you know about that?"

"Nothing. Like everyone else in Del, I believe that Endon is dead. That is what we were told."

"Indeed." Fallow paused. Then he leaned forward so that his face and the lighted torch were very close to the man on the floor. "Where is your son, Jarred?" he spat.

Lief's mouth went dry. He watched as his father

looked up. His heart ached as he saw the deep lines of exhaustion, pain, and grief on the well-loved face that was so like his own.

"Lief left our house months ago. The blacksmith's trade bored him. He preferred running wild with his friends in the city. We do not know where he is. Why do you ask about him? He broke his mother's heart, and mine."

Lief's own heart swelled at his father's courage. The voice was high and complaining — the voice of an injured parent, no more. His father, always so truthful, was lying as though he had been born to it, determined to protect his son, and his cause, at all costs.

Fallow was examining the despairing face closely. Was he deceived or not?

"It is said that a boy of about your son's age is one of the three criminals who are roving the land, trying to overturn the Master's plans," he said slowly. "With him are a girl and a grown man. A black bird flies with them."

"Why are you telling me this?" The man on the floor moved restlessly. He seemed to be merely impatient. But Lief, who knew him so well, could see that he had been listening intently. No doubt he was wondering furiously about this mention of a girl and a black bird. He knew nothing of Jasmine and Kree, or what had happened in the Forests of Silence.

"This boy," Fallow went on, "could be your son.

You are crippled, and may have sent him on some useless quest in your place. The man — could be Endon."

Lief's father laughed. The laugh sounded completely natural. As of course it would, Lief thought. It was absurd to think of Barda being mistaken for the delicate, cautious King Endon.

Fallow's thin lips set in a hard line. He lowered the flame of the torch till it flickered dangerously in front of the laughing man's eyes.

"Take good care, Jarred," he snarled. "Do not try my patience too far. Your life is in my hands. And not only yours."

The laughing stopped. Lief ground his teeth as he saw his father once again bow his head.

Fallow walked to the door. "I will be back," he said in a low voice. "Think over what I have said. The next time I come to see you, I will come expecting answers. If you have done what we suspect, mere pain will not make you tell the truth. But perhaps the pain of one you love will be more persuasive."

He lifted a fist and thumped on the door. It opened and he went through, banging it behind him. The key turned in the lock.

"Father!" Lief cried to the figure slumped against the wall. "Father, do not despair. We have four of the gems. And now we are going to Dread Mountain to find the fifth. We are moving as fast as we can!"

But his father sat motionless, staring unseeing

into the darkness. "They are alive," he whispered. "Alive, and succeeding!"

His eyes glowed. Chains rattled as he clenched his fists. "Oh, Lief, Barda — good fortune! I am fighting my fight here, as best I can. You must fight yours. My hopes and prayers go with you!"

6 - Take-off

Lief woke to the sound of voices. It was nearly dawn. Jasmine and Barda were already stirring, taking up their weapons, buckling the canisters of blisters to their belts. Ailsa, Merin, and Bruna were moving back from the spring. Lief lay still, remembering his dream. Though he must have slept for many hours after it was over, every detail was clear in his mind.

A terrible weight seemed to be pressing him down. It was the weight of his father's danger and pain, of fear for his mother. Then he remembered his father's glowing eyes, and those final words.

I am fighting my fight here, as best I can. You must fight yours . . .

Lief sat up, determinedly shaking off the misery.

"Jarred and Anna always knew that it might

come to this." Barda was standing beside him. His face was grim and drawn.

"You saw Father?" Lief exclaimed, jumping to his feet. "You too?"

They picked up their sleeping blankets, shouldered their packs, and began walking together to the spring, talking in low voices. Jasmine followed, listening.

"I dreamed as soon as I fell asleep," Barda said. "I knew you must be planning to do the same, Lief, but I wanted to see for myself how Jarred was faring. I learned little, but I saw him. He was sitting against the wall of a dungeon — in chains." His fists clenched at the memory. "I could do nothing. If only I could have told him — "

"He knows!" Lief exclaimed. "He knows we are succeeding. It has given him hope."

"He could *hear* you?"

"No. He found out another way."

They had reached the spring. As they breakfasted hastily on dried fruit and travellers' biscuits washed down with sweet water, Lief told of Fallow's visit to the cell. Barda laughed grimly when he heard that he was suspected of being King Endon.

"My dear old mother would be proud to hear it," he said. "So they have not noticed the disappearance of the beggar at the forge gates?"

"No," said Lief. "Or if they have, they think you have just moved elsewhere in the city." He frowned.

"But I am a different story. When trouble started they went to the forge, because of Father's history. They found I was gone. They searched the house . . ."

"And they found the book," muttered Barda. "I told Jarred long ago that he should destroy it. But he would not. He said it was too important."

Lief heard a small sound behind him and turned. Jasmine was pulling on her pack. Her mouth was set and her eyes sad. He thought he guessed why.

"I did not dream of anything last night," she said, in answer to his unspoken question. "I tried to picture my father as I drank from the spring, but I was so young when he was taken away that I cannot remember his face. It is just a blur to me now. So — I missed my chance."

"I am sorry," Lief murmured.

She shrugged, tossing her hair back. "Perhaps it is for the best. Father has been a prisoner for so many years. Who knows what he suffers? It would torment me, knowing I could do nothing to help him. It is better to think of him as dead, like my mother."

She turned away abruptly. "You had better make haste. We are losing time with this useless talk."

She walked off, with Kree flying beside her. Barda and Lief quickly packed up their own bags and followed. Both knew that great suffering lay behind Jasmine's harsh words. Both wished that they could help her.

But there was nothing to be done. Nothing to be

done for Jasmine, or her father, or Lief's parents, or any of the thousands of other victims of the Shadow Lord's cruelty. Except . . .

Except what we are doing now, Lief thought, as he approached the place beyond the grove where the Kin and Jasmine were waiting. The Belt of Deltora is our task. When that is complete — when Endon's heir has been found and the Shadow Lord overthrown — then all the prisoners will be free.

❋

The Kin were waiting beyond the trees, at the top of a grassy hill. They had all gathered to bid the travellers farewell, except Prin.

"Little One would not come," her mother explained. "I apologize for her. Usually she does not remain angry for long. This time it is different."

"This time the disappointment is very great," murmured Ailsa. "Poor Little One. I feel for her."

Merin glanced up at the lightening sky and turned to Barda. "As I am the largest, you are to ride with me," she said politely. Plainly, she was anxious to be gone.

Rather nervously, Barda climbed into her pouch. Lief had to smile at the sight, and despite their fears many of the watching Kin laughed aloud.

"What a large baby you have, Merin," called Prin's mother. "And how beautiful!"

Both Barda and Merin preserved a dignified silence.

Lief was to ride with Ailsa and Jasmine with Bruna, the smallest of the three. They climbed into the pouches in their turn, Filli chattering excitedly on Jasmine's shoulder. He plainly thought the Kin wonderful, and was thrilled to be so close to one.

Ailsa's pouch was warm and velvety soft. At first Lief was afraid that his weight would hurt her, but soon realized that his worry was needless. "A young Kin is far heavier than you by the time it leaves its mother's pouch for good," Ailsa told him. "Be comfortable."

But comfort was the last thing Lief felt shortly afterwards. He had wondered how such heavy creatures could leave the ground. Finding out at first hand was terrifying.

The method was quite simple. Ailsa, Merin, and Bruna stood in a line, spread their great wings, and then began running as fast as they could down the hill. Their passengers, jolted unmercifully, could only hold on, gasping for breath. Then they saw what was ahead. They were running straight for the edge of a cliff.

Lief yelled and shut his eyes as Ailsa launched herself into space. There were a few dizzy moments of panic as the great wings beat hard above his head. Then he felt an upward rush and a surge of cool air against his face. He realized that the sound of the wings had settled down to a steady beat. He opened his eyes.

The earth below looked like a patchwork rug embroidered all over with little trees and narrow winding paths. Ahead, Dread Mountain already seemed closer. It was still hazy, but looked larger, darker, and more ominous than it had before. Behind it were the folds of the mountain range that marked the border with the Shadowlands. They too seemed closer.

"How long will it take to reach the Mountain?" Lief shouted above the noise of the wind.

"We will have to stop when the light fails," Ailsa called back. "But if we continue to have good weather, we should reach it tomorrow."

Tomorrow! Lief thought. Tomorrow we will know for good or ill if the gnomes of Dread Mountain still watch the skies for Kin. If they do, it will mean our deaths. The gnomes will shoot down Ailsa, Merin, and Bruna, and we will go crashing to the ground with them.

He shivered. His hand stole down to the Belt at his waist and he lightly brushed the four gems set in place there. They warmed beneath his touch: the topaz for faith, the ruby for happiness, the opal for hope, and the mysterious lapis lazuli, the Heavenly Stone.

Surely all will be well, he told himself. Surely these gems together will keep us safe. But even as he thought this, words from *The Belt of Deltora* flashed into his mind.

✝   **Each gem has its own magic, but together the seven make a spell that is far more powerful than the sum of its parts. Only the Belt of Deltora, complete as it was first fashioned by Adin and worn by Adin's true heir, has the power to defeat the Enemy.**

The warning was clear. The gems that Lief and his companions had in their charge so far could help them on their way, but could not save them.

Lief took care not to let his fingers linger on the opal. He did not want to glimpse the future. If it was fearful, he did not wish to know it. He would face whatever fate had in store when the time came.

7 - Kinrest

As the sun sank in a blaze of red, the Kin circled lower and lower, searching for the place where they planned to spend the night.

"There is water there, and food, and shelter from above," Ailsa called to Lief. "It is a small forest where long ago we always broke our journey between the Mountain and the grove. We call it Kinrest."

It was almost dark by the time they dropped to earth, their great wings beating hard as they sank between tall trees to the soft shelter below.

Lief, Barda, and Jasmine climbed unsteadily to the ground. It felt very odd to have firm earth under their feet again. They looked around. Kinrest was indeed a peaceful place. Ferns thickly edged the small stream that bubbled through it, and toadstools grew in clumps under the great trees. Somewhere near there was the sound of a waterfall.

"How the trees have grown!" Merin exclaimed excitedly, brushing leaves and twigs from her fur. "They hide the stream completely. And, see, Ailsa — the entrance to the big cave where we used to play is choked with ferns."

"Everything looks quite different," Ailsa agreed. "No wonder we took so long to find it from above. We should have visited it in our dreams long ago, instead of always going to the Mountain."

Wearily Lief, Barda, and Jasmine sat down by the stream and watched as the three Kin began to explore. Jasmine put her head on one side, listening to the rustling of the trees.

"What do they say?" asked Lief eagerly. "Are we safe?"

Jasmine frowned. "I think so. The trees are happy to see Kin again. Many of them are hundreds of years old and remember past times clearly. But I sense sadness and fear in them also. Something bad happened here. Blood was spilled, and someone they cared for died."

"When?" demanded Barda, suddenly alert.

"Trees such as these do not speak of time as we do, Barda," Jasmine said patiently. "The sadness they are remembering could have happened one season ago or twenty. It is all one to them."

Suddenly she shivered. "I think it would be safe to light a small fire," she said. "The trees will surely hide the light. And I feel in need of cheer."

❋

The friends were crouching over the warming blaze of their fire, eating dried fruit and slices of nut and honey cake, when Ailsa called to them out of the dimness beyond the stream. Her voice sounded odd. Jumping up in alarm, they lit a torch and found their way to where she and the other Kin were standing by a large cave thickly overgrown with ferns.

"We were exploring our cave," Ailsa said in a low voice. "We used to play here as young ones. We found some — things inside it. We thought you would like to see them."

The three companions followed the Kin into the cave. The light of the torch flickered over the rocky walls and the sandy floor, showing the objects lying there: a few pots and pans, a mug, some old sleeping blankets lying on a bed of dust that had once been dried fern, a bundle of old clothes, a chair made of fallen branches, a dead torch fixed to a wall . . .

"Someone has been living here," breathed Lief.

"Not recently," Barda said, picking up a blanket and dropping it again in a cloud of dust. "Not for many years, I would say."

"There is something else," said Ailsa quietly.

She led them back to the cave entrance and parted the ferns that grew thickly on one side. A flat, mossy stone stood there, set firmly upright like a marker.

"There is writing scratched upon it," whispered Bruna.

Barda lowered the torch and the three companions saw that there were indeed words carved carefully into the stone.

HERE LIES DOOM
OF THE HILLS,
WHO SHELTERED
A FRIENDLESS
STRANGER AND SO
MET HIS DEATH.
HE WILL BE
AVENGED.

"A strange name to find on a gravestone," muttered Barda, glancing at Lief and Jasmine meaningfully. "And a strange message to go with it."

Stunned, Lief stared at the words. "Doom of the Hills is dead!" he breathed. "But this grave is old — ten years old at least, by the look of the stone. So the man *we* know as Doom — "

"Is someone else entirely," Jasmine finished crisply. Her face was flushed with anger. "He is going by a false name. I knew he could not be trusted. For all we know he is a Shadow Lord spy!"

"Do not be so foolish! That he does not use his real name proves nothing," growled Barda. "We ourselves were going by false names when we met him."

Lief nodded slowly. "He needed to conceal his identity. So he took the name of the man who lies buried in this place."

"A man he betrayed and murdered, perhaps," Jasmine muttered. "For he was here. I feel it!"

Barda would not answer her. Gently, he began to clear the ferns from around the stone. Lief bent to help him. Jasmine stood aside, her eyes cold and angry.

The three Kin looked helplessly on. Finally, Merin cleared her throat and clasped her paws. "It is clear that our find has caused you pain, and for that we are sorry," she said softly. "We have eaten many leaves, and drunk from the stream. Now we will curl, and sleep. We must leave early in the morning."

With that hint, she, Bruna, and Ailsa moved away and disappeared into the darkness. Shortly afterwards, Barda and Lief finished their work and moved back across the stream, with Jasmine silently following. By the time they reached the fire, the three Kin were huddled together, looking like a cluster of great rocks, and apparently fast asleep.

Lief wrapped himself in his sleeping blanket and

tried to sleep also. But suddenly the forest seemed less welcoming than it had before. A veil of sadness seemed to hang over the trees, and there were noises in the darkness: the breaking of twigs and the rustling of leaves, as though someone, or something, was watching them.

He could not help thinking about the man who called himself Doom. Despite what he had said to Jasmine, he had been shaken by the words on the gravestone. Doom had helped them, saved them from the Grey Guards. That was true. But had it been all part of a greater plot? A plot to gain their confidence? To worm from them the secret of their quest?

. . . *the Enemy is clever and sly, and to its anger and envy a thousand years is like the blink of an eye.*

Was it by chance that Doom had appeared in their lives once more? Or had he been acting under orders?

It does not matter. We told him nothing, Lief thought, pulling his blanket more tightly around him. But still doubts plagued him, and the night seemed to press in on him, the darkness full of mystery and menace.

Tonight we have all drunk from the stream, he told himself. We have not been drugged by the Dreaming Spring. We will wake if an enemy approaches. Kree is on the watch. And Jasmine says the trees feel we are safe.

But still it was a long time before he could sleep.

And when he did he dreamed of a lonely grave and a dark, bitter man whose face was hidden by a mask. Thick mist swirled about him, now parting, now closing in.

What was behind the mask? Was the man friend, or foe?

8 - The Mountain

The travellers set off again an hour before dawn, Ailsa, Bruna, and Merin leaping from the top of the waterfall to sail through a narrow valley and up into the skies once more. Now they were flying very fast. Their time at Kinrest seemed to have filled them with new energy.

"It is the stream water," Ailsa called to Lief. "For the first time in many years I slept without dreaming — or, at least, without the special dreams the spring gives. This morning I feel like a young one again."

"I too," called Bruna, who was flying beside them. "Though I did stir for a moment in the night. I thought I felt the tribe near. It seemed to me that they were trying to tell me something. But of course I could see and hear nothing, and the feeling soon passed."

She and Ailsa spoke no more, but Lief, watching

Dread Mountain growing larger on the horizon, felt worried. The Kin must have tried very hard to communicate with Bruna, for her to sense their presence. Could they have had news they needed to tell? Alarming news?

He closed his eyes and tried to force himself to relax. He would find out all too soon what Dread Mountain had in store.

※

By midday the Mountain was looming in front of them — a vast, dark mass filling their view. Its jagged surface was thick with cruel rocks and prickly dark green trees. Clouds were gathering around its peak. A road wound away from its base, disappearing into the range of peaks beyond. The road to the Shadowlands, Lief thought, his stomach churning.

It was impossible to see through the leaves of the thickly clustered trees. Even now the gnomes could have sighted them. They could be hiding, deadly arrows aimed, waiting for the three Kin to come within range. Lief's eyes strained for a glimpse of metal glinting, any sign of movement. He could see nothing, but still he feared.

"This is the dangerous time," Ailsa called to him. "I must begin making it harder for the gnomes to take aim. I was taught to do this long ago, but it is not something you forget. Hold tight!"

She began swooping and wheeling, zooming upward, dropping again. Gasping, holding on for dear life, Lief saw that Merin and Bruna were following Ailsa's lead, making the same sudden movements.

And just in time. Moments later, the first arrow sped towards them, just missing Ailsa. A faint chorus of shrill cries sounded from below. Lief looked down, and his skin crawled. Suddenly the rocks were covered by pale-skinned, hollow-eyed creatures, every one with a fiercely grinning face and a drawn bow. Suddenly hundreds of arrows were hurtling towards them like deadly, upward-flying rain.

Left, right, up, down swooped Ailsa, dodging and swerving but all the time moving forward. Closer they came to the Mountain, and closer, till it seemed that the tops of the trees were rushing to meet them, till it seemed that surely one of the arrows must find its mark.

"All the gnomes are up high, near their stronghold!" Bruna cried. "Land lower down, Kin, lower, where the Boolong trees are thickest. They will not venture there."

The air was filled with the gnomes' high, gobbling shrieks and the soft grunts of the Kin as they threw their huge bodies this way and that. Lief could hear Ailsa's heart pounding, and, faintly, the shouts of Barda and Jasmine, urging Merin and Bruna on.

"Cover your face!" bellowed Ailsa. And with a crash they hit the treetops, smashing through leaves and branches, shattering all in their path to the ground.

※

"Lief, are you all right?"

Stiffly, Lief uncovered his face and blinked into Ailsa's dark, anxious eyes. He swallowed. "I am very well, thank you," he croaked. "As well as anyone can be who has just crashed through a thorn tree."

Ailsa nodded solemnly. "It was not my best landing," she agreed. "But there are no gaps in the Boolongs here. That is why we are safe from the gnomes. They do not like the thorns."

"I do not love them myself," grunted Barda, who was sitting on the ground beside Jasmine, inspecting several wicked-looking scratches on the backs of his hands. He hauled himself to his feet, went to a narrow stream that gurgled nearby, and began bathing the wounds.

Merin and Bruna had plunged into the thick of the gnarled trees that overhung the trickling water. They were joyously pulling hard little black cones from the clusters of prickly leaves that grew all over the twisted trunks, and crunching them as though they were sweets.

"So these are Boolong trees," Barda went on. "I cannot say I find them pleasing. I have never seen such spines."

"They do not hurt us," said Ailsa. She picked a few clinging leaves from her velvety fur, popped them into her mouth, and chewed with relish, despite the long, needle-sharp thorns at their edges.

54

"When we lived here there were not so many Boolong trees, and there were many paths winding through them," she went on, with her mouth full. "The streams were wide, and there were clearings everywhere. Without us to feed on them, the Boolongs have grown and spread wonderfully. The cones are full of seed, of course. That is what makes them so tasty!"

Above, there was the rumble of thunder. Ailsa stopped chewing and sniffed the air. Then she hurried over to where Merin and Bruna were still thrashing around, feasting. "We must go!" the companions heard her calling. "A storm is coming. Fill your pouches with cones. We will take them home for the others."

Jasmine shook her head. "The gnomes must have the gem. But I do not know how we are to climb to their stronghold through this thorn forest," she muttered. "We will be cut to pieces if we try. We can only sit here now because the Kin smashed a clearing when they landed."

"Perhaps we could clear a path with fire," Lief suggested.

Kree squawked, Filli chattered nervously, and Jasmine shook her head.

"That would be far too dangerous," she said. "We could never control a fire in woods as thick as these. The blaze could easily burn us all."

The three Kin came towards them, their pouches

bulging with cones and bundles of thorny leaves. They looked as though they had been arguing.

"We came to say farewell," Ailsa said. "We must leave now, so as to be away before the storm breaks. Storms here are fierce and can last for days."

"We should not leave our friends alone so soon!" Merin exclaimed. "There is too much they do not know."

Bruna's whiskers twitched crossly. "Merin, we promised Crenn that we would return as quickly as possible. And if we are marooned here — "

"We would not be marooned!" Merin exclaimed. "This is our place. This is where we should be, for always. I see that, now that I am here." Her eyes were bright with excitement. "We should stay, and the others can join us. The gnomes cannot touch us here, in the lower part of the Mountain."

"Merin, we landed safely by a miracle," Ailsa sighed. "Do you want our friends to take that risk? How many do you think would survive?"

"And even if only half did so," Bruna put in, "the Boolong trees would be eaten back to normal in a few years. Then the paths would be open once more, the gnomes would come back, and the slaughter would start again."

Merin hung her head. "It is cruel," she whispered. But Lief, Barda, and Jasmine could see that she knew her friends were right.

Overhead, the thunder growled. Ailsa glanced nervously at the sky. "There is a big outcrop of rock not far from here," she said rapidly. "I saw it as we landed. It will be quickest if we take off from there. It will be heavy work, but I think we are all strong enough to do it."

With Lief, Barda, and Jasmine following, the three Kin pushed a track up through the Boolong trees. Soon they had reached the rocks and were looking out at open sky. Dark clouds had rolled in from the south.

"The clouds will hide us, once we are safely inside them," Ailsa said. "And if I am right the gnomes will not be looking down here. They will be watching higher up, hoping for more of us to arrive."

"Farewell, then, good Kin," said Barda. "We cannot thank you enough for what you have done for us."

"There is no need for thanks," Bruna answered simply. "All of us are richer for seeing our home again — even for this little time. All we ask is that you take care so that one day we may see you again."

The three bent, touching their heads to Lief's, Barda's, and Jasmine's foreheads. Then they turned, spread their wings, and sprang for the sky.

For a few tense moments, wings beating frantically, they struggled just to stop themselves from crashing back down to earth. The companions watched in breathless silence, sure that at any moment the gnomes would hear the wing beats, look down, fire . . .

But all was well. There were no shouts, no arrows shooting from above, as the Kin at last steadied and began moving forward. Their outlines grew fainter as the clouds closed in around them. Then they were gone.

Barda turned away with a sigh of relief and began scrambling back down the rocks. Lief was about to follow when he caught sight of something out of the corner of his eye. He looked up and to his amazement saw a dark shape emerging unsteadily from the clouds above their heads.

"One of the Kin is returning!" he breathed. "But why so high? Oh, no!"

All of them stared up, aghast, at the Kin blundering into view right in the gnomes' firing line. It was not Ailsa, Bruna, or Merin. It was . . .

"Prin!" hissed Lief in terror.

The little Kin caught sight of the patch of broken trees that marked the others' landing place. She began flying towards it, stubby wings flapping weakly. The next moment there was a high, triumphant shriek and a gale of laughter from further up the Mountain, something was hurtling through the air, and Prin was falling, falling, with an arrow in her chest.

9 ~ Fear

Crying out in horror, Lief, Barda, and Jasmine leaped from the rock and pounded down to the clearing. Prin was struggling feebly on the ground by the stream. Her wings were crumpled beneath her and she was making small, piteous sounds. Her eyes were glazed with pain.

The arrow that had pierced her chest had already fallen out. The wound it had left was small. But the poison the arrow carried had acted swiftly, and its terrible work was nearly done. Prin's agonized eyes closed.

"Foolish child!" groaned Barda. "Jasmine, the — "

"The nectar — " cried Lief at the same moment. But Jasmine was already tearing the tiny jar from around her neck and tipping it over the little Kin's chest. The last golden drops of the nectar of the Lilies of Life fell into the wound. Three drops — no more.

"If this is not enough, there is nothing more we can do," Jasmine muttered, shaking the jar to show that it was empty. She ground her teeth in anger. "Oh, what did they suppose they would gain, shooting at her? They knew she must fall down here, where they could not get to her. Do they kill just for enjoyment?"

"It seems they do," said Barda. "Did you not hear them laughing?"

Lief cradled Prin's head in his arms, calling her back to life as once he had called Barda in the Forests of Silence. As Jasmine had called Kree on the way to the Lake of Tears. As Lief himself had been called in the City of the Rats. The nectar that Jasmine had caught as it dripped from the blooming Lilies of Life so long ago had saved three lives. Would it save another?

Prin stirred. Lief held his breath as the small wound on her chest began to close up and disappear. Her eyes opened. She blinked, looking up at Lief in surprise.

"Did I fall?" she asked.

"Prin, what are you *doing* here?" thundered Lief.

He saw her shrink back and cursed himself, realizing that he had fallen into the trap of letting fear and relief make him angry. Barda had done this not so long ago, in the Shifting Sands, and Lief had resolved that he would never do the same. So much for resolutions, he thought grimly.

"I am sorry, Prin," he said in a gentler voice. "I did not mean to shout. But we have been so afraid for you. Have you flown all this way alone?"

Prin nodded, still eyeing him warily. "I followed you," she said. "I could not bear to miss my only chance to see the Mountain."

She looked around the clearing, drinking in the sight. Her voice was growing stronger by the moment. "I slept near you at Kinrest, and you never knew," she went on gleefully. "But today the others flew so fast that I fell behind. I was so, so tired. And then the clouds came, and I was lost. Then — "

Her eyes widened in sudden terror. She clutched at her chest. Then she looked down and gasped as she saw that there was no wound to be seen.

"I thought I was hurt," she whispered. "But — it must have been a dream."

The companions glanced at one another. "It was no dream," said Lief gently. "You were wounded. But we had — a potion that made you well again."

"You should not have come, Prin," growled Barda. "What would your tribe do if they lost you, their only young one?"

"I knew I would not be lost," said Prin confidently. She clambered to her feet and looked around. "Where is Ailsa?" she asked, bouncing up and down. "And Merin, and Bruna? They will be very surprised to see me! They did not think I could fly so far."

Without waiting for an answer she jumped across the stream and began thrashing around in the trees on the other side, calling.

"She does not realize they have gone," Barda muttered to Lief and Jasmine. "No doubt she expected to return home with them. She will never find her way back alone. Whatever are we to do with her?"

"She will have to come with us," Jasmine said calmly.

"But it is too dangerous!" Lief exclaimed.

Jasmine shrugged. "She chose to come here. She must put up with what happens as a result. The Kin spoil her, and treat her as a baby. But she is not a baby. She is young, but not helpless. She can be useful to us."

She nodded over to where Prin was dancing in the stream, breaking off cones and leaves from the overhanging Boolong trees and eating ravenously. Already the little Kin had cleared a broad space among the prickles.

"You see? She can help us make a path," Jasmine said. "If we follow the stream — "

"It is out of the question," Barda broke in firmly. "I refuse to be burdened by another wilful child who has more energy than sense. Two are quite enough!"

Lief did not take offense at the grim joke as once he would have done, but he did not smile either. The idea of taking Prin up the Mountain was as unpleasing to him as it was to Barda.

Thunder growled above their heads. It had grown very dim in the clearing. The air was thick and heavy.

"Our first task must be to find some shelter," Jasmine said. "The storm — " Suddenly she stiffened, her head on one side. She was listening intently.

"What . . . ?" Lief began softly. Then he realized that the sound of the stream had become louder. It was rising every moment. In seconds it was as though water was rushing towards the clearing. A flood? he thought, confused. But there has been no rain yet, and in any case the sound is coming from downhill. How — ?

Then he forgot everything as he saw Prin standing quite still in the middle of the stream, staring, startled, in the direction of the rushing sound.

"Prin!" he shouted. "Get out! Get out!"

Prin squeaked and half-flew, half-sprang, out of the water and onto the bank. At the same moment there was a roar, and a huge, glistening man-shaped horror came leaping into view, landing exactly where the little Kin had been standing and missing her by a hair. Growling in anger at having been cheated of its prize, the thing swung around, raising its ghastly head.

"Vraal!" Prin shrieked, her voice cracking in terror as she stumbled backwards away from the stream. "Vraal!"

Lief's blood ran cold as he grabbed for his

63

sword. The Vraal's snakelike scales, dull green striped with yellow, shone evilly in the weak forest light. It was as tall as Barda and twice as wide, with hulking, bowed shoulders, a lashing tail, and powerful arms that ended in claws like curved knives. But the most horrible thing about it was that it seemed to have no face — just a lumpy, scaly mass of flesh, with no eyes, nose, or mouth.

Then it roared. The mass seemed to split in half like an exploding fruit as its jaws gaped red. At the same moment its eyes became visible — burning orange slits glaring through protective ridges and folds. It leaped from the stream, landing on the bank in a single movement.

Now Lief could see that instead of feet it had cloven hoofs that dug deeply into the soft, damp earth. They seemed too delicate to support such a huge body, but as it roared again and sprang forward, Lief put this thought out of his mind.

The creature was a killing machine. That was clear as day. It took no notice of the thunder that rumbled above the trees. Its evil eyes were fixed on Prin.

"Prin! Down!" roared Barda's voice. Terrified into instant obedience, Prin threw herself to the ground as a blister flew above her head towards the Vraal. Barda had hurled the weapon with all his strength, but the creature leaped aside with astounding speed and the blister smashed harmlessly into a tree, the poison inside hissing as it trickled to the ground.

Cursing, Barda threw another blister — the last he had, Lief saw in terror. The big man's aim was true, but again the creature leaped aside just in time, its hoofs digging great holes in the earth, landing firmly in another place. A place away from Prin, but closer to Barda.

Lief saw Prin scramble away and roll into the stream. She would not be safe there! He wanted to call to her to run, but did not want to turn the creature's attention to her. Then, as he hesitated, he realized that the Vraal had forgotten all about the little Kin. Its orange eyes were burning as it turned to face the man it now saw as its chief enemy. The man who had tried to kill it with Grey Guards' poison. The man who now stood facing it, sword drawn.

The creature's lipless mouth stretched in a hideous grin and it hissed as it stretched out its claws, daring Barda to fight.

10 - Fight

B arda stood his ground. He knew that to turn, to step aside, to show any fear at all, would be fatal. Behind him, Lief and Jasmine glanced at each other. The creature moved like lightning. The remaining blisters, which were in Jasmine's keeping, were useless while Barda stood between her and the enemy. The only hope was for her to creep to one side without being seen.

Without warning, the Vraal lashed out. Barda's sword flew up in defense and the creature's claws rang against the shining steel. Barda twisted and lunged, and this time the Vraal defended, hitting the flat of the sword with such a mighty thump that Barda staggered.

Lief sprang to his friend's side, his own sword held high. The Vraal hissed with pleasure. Two foes were even better than one. It had not fought for a long, long time, and fighting was what it had been bred for.

It had missed using its skills. It had missed the joy of battle and the screams of defeated enemies. Snatching squealing, wriggling gnomes from the stream as they bent to drink was no sport. Dodging arrows was too easy. But this — this warmed its cold blood.

Growling, it sprang at the two swords, beating them away effortlessly, driving the two weaklings who held them back, and back. Twice the weapons pierced its armoured skin. It cared nothing for that. It cared nothing for the black bird that dived at its head, snapping with sharp beak then wheeling to dive again.

The Vraal did not fear pain, did not fear death. Its mind was not fitted for such thoughts, or indeed any thoughts but one — that any creatures not of its own species were enemies, to be fought and defeated. In the Shadow Arena or here — it did not matter.

Once only in its life had it lost a fight. But that was long ago, in the Shadowlands. The Vraal no longer remembered the loss, or the pursuit that had left it marooned and wandering in this place. It no longer remembered the Guards who had accompanied it. Their gnawed bones had sunk beneath the earth of the forest long ago. The steel ring that hung from the back of its neck was all that remained of its old life. That, and the need to kill.

It saw that the third enemy, the small female with the dagger in one hand and Guards' poison in the other, was edging from behind the others, moving away. She was going to attack from the side, or from behind. She was moving slowly, carefully. She thought the Vraal, occupied with her companions, would not notice her. She was wrong. It would deal with her presently.

The Vraal sprang suddenly, slashed, and with satisfaction saw the smaller of the two swordsmen falter, and smelled fresh, red blood. The smell stirred vague memories of times long past. Gnomes' blood was thin and bitter, like stale green water. This was better. Much better.

The little one, the female, was clear of the others now. Where was she? The Vraal opened one of its side eyes. Deeply buried in ridges of scaly skin over its ear slits, the side eyes did not see quite as well as the eyes at the front, but they were useful.

Ah, yes, there she was. Raising her arm, taking aim. Time to dispatch her. A single lash of the tail . . . there!

As the female fell, the black bird flying above her head screeched and the injured swordsman cried out — a single word. The Vraal understood few words and did not know this one, but it knew fear and grief when it heard them. The Vraal grinned, its mouth stretching wide.

"Jasmine!" Lief shouted again. But Jasmine lay

where she had fallen, silent and still as death.

Barda cried out in warning. Lief ducked the Vraal's swinging claws just in time and staggered, falling backwards, hitting the ground hard. He scrambled to his knees. His head was pounding. The breath was sobbing in his throat. Blood was streaming from the long cut in his arm. He could barely hold his sword.

"Lief," panted Barda, leaping in front of him and beating the Vraal back as it lunged again, kicking with hard, deadly hooves. "Go! Get the Belt away!"

"I will not leave you," Lief gasped. "And Jasmine — "

"Do as I tell you!" Barda roared savagely. "You are injured. No use to either of us. Get away! Now!"

Furiously he swung his great sword, attacking with all his strength, pushing the Vraal back one step . . . two.

Lief began to crawl painfully away. Spines from the fallen, smashed Boolong trees pierced his hands, stinging and burning. He staggered to his feet and took a few more steps. Then he stopped and turned.

Flight was useless. There was nowhere to go, nowhere to hide. When the Vraal had finished with Barda it would come after him. Better, surely, to die fighting here than to die cringing among the Boolong trees, crushed into the thorns.

A flash of lightning lit the clearing for an instant, showing the scene in hideous clarity. Barda battling with the gleaming, hulking Vraal, Jasmine lying motionless on the ground. And Prin . . . Prin toiling from the stream, her eyes enormous with fear, her front paws clasped together in front of her, clutching a mess of purple slime. As Lief watched, amazed, she spread her wings.

Then the air exploded with a terrible clap of thunder. The very earth seemed to shake. Barda faltered, lost his footing, and fell to one knee. The Vraal sprang, its slitted orange eyes gleaming. With one swipe of its huge arm it beat away the big man's sword. The gleaming steel turned in the air, once, twice, and fell to the ground far out of reach, its point buried in the earth. The Vraal hissed, grinning, preparing for the kill.

"Barda!" Lief cried out in agony. He staggered forward. But Prin — suddenly Prin was springing forward and up, straight at the Vraal, landing squarely on the back of its neck and clinging there, slime-filled paws wrapped around its head, wings flapping wildly.

The Vraal roared and staggered. Its terrible claws flailed around its head, now smeared all over with purple. Prin leaped backwards, landing on her strong back legs and stumbling back to the stream, her paws, still purple-streaked, held out in front of her.

"No, Prin! Run into the trees! It will see you there!" shouted Lief.

But he was wrong. The Vraal was seeing nothing. It threw back its head, screaming in rage and pain.

"It is the moss!" sobbed Prin, frantically washing her paws. "In its eyes, its ears! The purple moss! The green moss cures, the purple moss harms. They told me! They told me so often, and it is true!"

Lightning flashed and there was another huge clap of thunder. Then, as if the sky had cracked open, rain began pelting down — hard, icy rain mixed with hail. Barda staggered to his feet and stumbled towards his sword. Lief also gathered his wits and started forward. On the ground, Jasmine stirred as Kree screeched frantically.

But the Vraal had had enough. With a final roar it turned and, as Prin jumped aside, it blundered blindly to the stream, fell into it, and splashed away.

✳

Later, soaked, exhausted, and chilled to the bone, the companions crouched together in the shelter of a small cave made by a rock that overhung the stream. Stinging hail still pounded the earth outside. They had managed to light a fire, but so far it was doing little to warm them. There was not one of them, however, who felt like complaining.

"I thought our hour had come," said Barda, lighting a torch by dipping it into the fire. "That beast would not have stopped until all of us were dead. Lief — how is your arm?"

"It feels much better already," Lief said. He was

lying with his back propped against his pack. His injured arm was bound with what looked like a green bandage, but was in fact clumps of green moss taken fresh from the stream and tied in place with vines.

Having seen the moss's effect on the Vraal, and the terrible blisters it had raised on Prin's paws, Lief had at first been unwilling to have it near him. But Prin had assured him that the moss in its green state had amazing healing powers, and to prove it she had padded her own burned skin with the stuff, and asked Jasmine to bind it on tightly.

"Often I have heard the others speak of the green-purple moss," she said now, as Barda raised the torch to send light and shadows leaping around the cave. "The gnomes use it for their wounds, and Kin who were injured by Vraal in the old days could be saved by green moss also. It is only when the moss is old and water-soaked, when it has fallen under the edge of the rocks that line the stream and has turned purple, that it clings and burns. Of course, it is not a real poison, like the gnomes use on their arrows. It only troubles Vraal in their eyes and ears. And even they recover quickly. Our Vraal will be ready to fight again in a few days."

Lief glanced at her. She smiled at him, her padded paws tucked into her pouch for warmth and comfort. "You were very brave, Prin," he said. "You saved us all. Your people would be very proud of you."

"Indeed," Jasmine said warmly, and Filli chattered agreement.

Prin sat up a little straighter. "The Kin have always used the purple moss to defend themselves from the Vraal and Grey Guards who used to come here in great numbers," she said, plainly proud of her knowledge. "Mother and Crenn have told me about it, many times."

"I wonder then that Ailsa, Bruna, and Merin did not show it to us," Jasmine said, frowning.

Prin shook her head. "In their dreaming they have never seen a prowling Vraal, or a Grey Guard either," she said. "In the mornings they speak only of the Boolong trees. They think the gnomes are the only dangers on the Mountain now."

"Perhaps that is the trouble with dreaming," Barda said slowly. "You see only what the dream shows you, and then for only a little time. For example, did your people ever tell you, Prin, of seeing a traveller of our kind on the Mountain?"

The little Kin shook her head. "They say no one comes here now. They say the gnomes' poison arrows keep everyone away."

"Not everyone, it seems," said Barda quietly. He jerked his head towards the back of the cave and held the torch high.

Everyone turned to look. Lief drew a sharp breath. There were faded words on the pale, soft stone. Written, Lief was sure, in blood:

WHO AM I?
ALL IS DARKNESS. BUT I
WILL NOT DESPAIR.
THREE THINGS I KNOW;
I KNOW I AM A MAN.
I KNOW WHERE I HAVE BEEN.
I KNOW WHAT I MUST DO.
FOR NOW, THAT IS ENOUGH.

11 - Mysteries

Lief, Barda, and Jasmine stared at the scrawled words on the cave wall. All of them were imagining the lonely, suffering man who, it seemed, had used his own blood to write the message.

Why had he written it? To keep himself sane, perhaps, thought Lief. To convince himself that, in the nightmare of terror and confusion that his life had become, some things were real. That he himself was real.

"Who was he?" breathed Jasmine. "Where is he now?"

"Dead, perhaps," said Barda. "If he was wounded, then — "

"He did not die here, at least, for the cave is empty of bones," Lief broke in. "Perhaps he recovered, and escaped from the Mountain." He found himself hoping against hope that this was so.

"He says, 'I know where I have been,' " Jasmine

murmured. "Surely that means that he came here from somewhere else, not long before he wrote the message."

"He could have come from the Shadowlands, like the Vraal," Prin put in helpfully.

"That is impossible. No one escapes from the Shadowlands," Barda growled.

Lief leaned back, his head suddenly swimming. He felt Jasmine's hand on his arm and struggled to look at her.

"You have lost much blood, Lief," she said, in a voice that sounded far away. "That is why you feel weak. Do not fight the urge to sleep. Barda and I will keep watch. Do not fear."

Lief wanted to speak — to tell her that he too would take his turn to keep watch. To say that she had been knocked unconscious by the Vraal and was also in need of rest. To beg her to make sure that Prin stayed safe. But his eyelids would not stay open, and his mouth would not form the words. So at last he simply did as she asked, and slept.

✳

The storm raged on all that night and through the next day. Thunder roared without ceasing. The hail became icy rain. Wind lashed the Boolong trees, and many crashed to the ground.

The companions could do nothing but stay huddled in their shelter, eating, resting, drinking from the stream that rushed by the cave's opening, taking turns

76

to keep watch. By the time night fell again they were fretting about the delay. Lief's arm and Prin's paws were healing wonderfully, and they feared that the Vraal might be recovering just as quickly.

"Only if it has learned that the green moss heals," Prin reminded them, nibbling a Boolong cone. "And I do not think that is likely. Vraal are clever only in fighting and killing, Mother says."

At the mention of her mother her voice faltered, and she swallowed hard.

"It is very fortunate for us that you were with us when the Vraal came. But your mother, and the other Kin, must be worried about you, Prin," said Lief after a moment.

"They know I am safe," Prin said softly. "I am sure they visited us last night, in their dreams."

She looked around. "And now it is night again. They could be here at this very moment. They would all fit, because, after all, it is only a dream." She bent her head. "If they *were* here, I would tell them I was sorry for causing them pain," she murmured. "And I would say I missed them very much."

The others were silent. It was eerie to think that they might be surrounded by Kin spirits, yearning to speak to Prin, to touch her, but unable to do so. It was sad to realize that Prin was deliberately saying aloud the words she wanted her family to hear, just in case.

✳

By the following morning, the wind had died and the storm had retreated, leaving steady, light rain in its place. The travellers decided that it was time to move on.

They began climbing through the rain in single file, following the swollen stream, alert for the sound of the gnomes above them and the Vraal below. The way was steep, slippery, and dangerous. Prin went first, doing the best she could to beat a safe path, but despite her best efforts the companions were soon covered in scratches.

After an hour or two of this miserable tramping, the rain stopped and a few weak rays of sun began to struggle through the clouds.

"That is something, at least," muttered Barda. Then he jumped as Prin stopped suddenly in front of him and darted off the path.

"What is it?" whispered Jasmine from behind.

"I do not know!" Barda whispered back irritably. "Prin! What are you doing?"

Prin had disappeared into the trees and was thrashing around, breaking down branches with new energy and purpose. "Come and see!" she called softly to them, after a moment.

Unwillingly, shielding their faces from the thorns, they crept into the small, cleared area she had made. Then they stopped, staring.

Right in the center of the clearing was a small round stone hut roofed with bark. Two rusted metal spikes stood on either side of the low door, each crowned by a grinning skull. To the door itself was fixed a beaten metal shape.

"I am sure this is a gnome-rest," Prin whispered. "The huts where gnomes shelter if they are caught out in storms. They are forbidden to strangers. That is what the sign means. But — "

She looked at them anxiously.

"But this has been abandoned for a very long time," Barda reassured her. "You were right to uncover it." He strode to the door and pulled at it. It sagged open and the companions went inside.

If they had hoped to find weapons, they were disappointed. The little building was festooned with webs and crawling with spiders and beetles. Otherwise it was empty except for a few mugs, some woven rugs which had almost rotted away, and a pile of what had probably once been food, but which was now black dust.

"It is strange," murmured Prin, as they backed out again with relief. "Mother told me that in the old days there were gnome-rests scattered all over the Mountain, all of them linked by paths that crisscrossed everywhere. But this is the first gnome-rest we have seen, and it was completely overgrown by the trees."

Lief looked around at the dark and silent forest that surrounded the clearing. "The Boolong trees have run wild since the Kin left. But that cannot be the only reason why the gnomes have abandoned their buildings and their paths. Surely they would have fought to save some of them, at least."

Jasmine too had been looking around her. "Something else has happened. Some change we do not know about," she said slowly.

There was a sound behind them. Prin glanced over her shoulder nervously, then gave a start. Barda had begun pulling sheets of bark from the roof of the little hut. Already three large pieces lay beside him on the ground.

"Oh, do not do that!" she begged, hurrying over to him. "The gnomes will be angry. Do you not see their warning sign?"

"I care nothing for that," snorted Barda, pulling a fourth sheet onto the ground. "They have already shown they are our enemies. In any case, they have plainly abandoned this hut to the forest. And this bark will be very useful to us."

Prin stared at him, and Lief and Jasmine also raised their eyebrows in surprise. Smiling, Barda tapped the bark sheets with his foot. "This is Boolong bark," he said. "See how hard it is? Yet it is light to carry, and slightly curved too. With vines to bind them, these pieces will make excellent shields. Shields that will stop any arrow — and will protect us from the Boolong thorns."

They spent the next half hour binding vine strongly around the bark pieces so that they could be held easily from the back. Standing behind their shields' protection all the companions felt safer.

"You must always carry your shield in your weaker hand," Barda instructed. "Then your strong hand is left free for fighting. It is tiring at first, but you will soon get used to — "

He broke off, startled, as Jasmine suddenly jumped up and raised her finger to her lips. "I hear voices," she breathed. "And feet. Marching feet."

Lief and Barda listened carefully and at last heard a faint, buzzing, rhythmic sound, like harsh chanting or singing, coming from further down the Mountain.

"Gnomes," whimpered Prin.

The sound was coming closer, growing louder by the moment.

12 - The Way Up

They pushed deep into the trees and crouched together in a tight circle, their shields held up around them like a wall. The sound of gruff singing and feet marching in time grew louder. Yet there was no noise of cracking branches or of weapons slashing at spiny leaves, and the marching feet did not hesitate as they passed by somewhere just out of sight.

"There must be a road nearby," Barda breathed.

As the singing began to fade away into the distance, the companions crept from their hiding place and began forcing a path in the direction from which the sound had come. Sure enough, in a short time they found themselves standing on a narrow track that wound away towards the top. It was so overhung with tree branches that it was like a tunnel.

Lief groaned. "We might have known that the

gnomes would keep at least one path clear. No doubt this trail leads all the way from the bottom of the Mountain to the top! If only we had found it before!"

"That troop of gnomes must have been at the bottom of the Mountain before the storm struck," Barda said. "I wonder what business they had there? Bad business, I suspect, for the only thing at the Mountain's base is the road to the Shadowlands."

"But the gnomes are not friends of the Grey Guards," squeaked Prin, speaking up for the first time since they heard the sound of marching feet. "They hate them, and plague them with evil tricks. Mother told me about it often. Those skulls by the gnome-rest — they are probably Guards' skulls."

"Many years have passed since your mother lived on Dread Mountain, Prin," Lief said gently. "Now the gnomes are allies of the Shadow Lord."

Prin shook her head, but perhaps the last few days had helped her to grow up a little, because she did not go on arguing, insisting that she was right. Instead she simply gripped her shield more firmly and followed as the companions began the long climb towards the Mountain top.

✳

The sun was going down and it was growing very cold when finally they reached the end of the road. The climb had been hard, but without trouble of any kind. Not a single gnome had crossed their path. And now, as they peered cautiously around the last bend, they could see no sign of life or movement. All was utterly still.

"Where are they hiding? Be ready. We may be walking into a trap," muttered Barda. But nothing stirred, and no arrows flew, as they began to cross the cleared space beyond the road, looking up at the towering cliff of rock that now barred their way.

There were no trees here. The earth on which they walked was bare, white chalky stuff, packed hard by the tread of feet, littered with discarded arrows. The top of the Mountain, hidden in swirling clouds, was still high above their heads.

Jasmine summoned Kree to her shoulder and drew her dagger. "It is some sort of trick," she whispered. "The gnomes we heard could not have disappeared. And the others — the ones who shot at us when we landed — were here. Somewhere, they are waiting."

The cliff rose dark and ominous before them. At first they could see nothing odd about it except for a few small holes dotted over its surface. But as soon as they drew close enough, they saw where the gnomes had gone.

There was a narrow door in the cliff, carved from solid rock. It was dark at the top, light at the bottom. No attempt had been made to disguise it — in fact, the larger pale section had been decorated with grooved lines, and at one side there was a round stone doorknob which had a deep carving in the shape of an arrow in its center. But the knob would not turn, and pull and push as they would, the door would not open.

"Gnome tricks!" growled Barda, running his fingers over the stone and pressing vainly here and there.

"Why do you want to get in?" Prin whispered nervously. "Surely this is the gnomes' stronghold. Where they eat and sleep. And where they keep their treasure."

"Exactly," Barda frowned, still testing the stone.

"The decorations are only on the bottom part of the door, the light part," said Lief. "That may be a clue."

He moved very close to the cliff and peered at the seemingly empty space at the top of the door. The dark, uneven rock blurred before his eyes, but he was sure he could make out marks that were not natural.

"There is something carved here," he muttered. "Words, I think. But they are so small, and the rock is so dark, that I cannot make them out."

He pulled his cloak and his shirt aside to uncover the Belt of Deltora and noticed at once that the ruby's rich red had faded to dull pink — a sign that danger threatened. I do not need warning of that, he thought grimly. I know only too well that we are going into danger.

His fingers moved towards the topaz. It had sharpened his wits before. Perhaps it would help him now.

But before he had even touched the gem an idea came to him. He bent, scraped up a handful of the white dust beneath his feet, and smeared it over the dark rock. Then he brushed the loose dust away. The dust that remained caught in the carved letters made them show quite clearly:

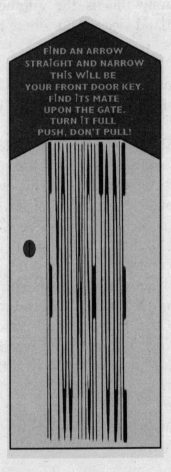

FIND AN ARROW
STRAIGHT AND NARROW
THIS WILL BE
YOUR FRONT DOOR KEY.
FIND ITS MATE
UPON THE GATE.
TURN IT FULL
PUSH, DON'T PULL!

"This rhyme is very childish," frowned Jasmine. "It reminds me of rhymes my father taught me when I was very young. And it was not difficult to make the words visible. These gnomes are not so clever."

"They are careless too," said Barda, picking up an arrow from the ground. "If arrows are keys to their door, they should not leave them lying around. And as for finding the arrow's mate upon the gate . . ."

He dug the point of the arrow into the carving on the doorknob. The arrow slid into place easily, like a key slipping into a lock. As Barda had suspected, there was a keyhole at the bottom of the carving. Gripping the shaft of the arrow firmly, he turned it until there was a slight but definite click.

"It is unlocked. Shall we go in?" he asked, turning to his companions and drawing his sword.

"No!" Prin begged, unable to keep silent any longer. "You say the gnomes are not clever, but they are, they are! They love tricks and traps. This is their door. If we use it we will die. I know it!"

"We must enter the stronghold, Prin," said Lief firmly. "The gnomes have something hidden here that we must find. But you need not enter with us. You can return to the path and keep watch."

He drew his own sword and nodded to Barda, who began to push firmly on the door. With a harsh, grating sound, the great piece of stone began to swing inward.

And just then Lief thought he heard, from somewhere high above them, a muffled giggle. He grasped Barda's arm and held it. "Wait!" he hissed.

Jasmine had heard the sound too. She was looking up, peering intently at the cliff face. "There is no one to be seen," she whispered. "But I am sure I heard someone laugh."

"It was a birdcall, perhaps," said Barda. He stood, undecided, his hand still on the door.

Kree squawked.

"It was not a bird," Jasmine said flatly. "It was someone laughing. At us."

They stood in tense silence for a moment, listening. But once again the Mountain was utterly still, as though it was waiting.

Barda shrugged, grasped his sword more tightly, and pushed the door again. The grating sound grew louder as the slab of rock moved inward. A narrow gap appeared between the door and the cliff wall. From somewhere beyond the gap, light flickered.

Jasmine peered through the crack. "I can see no one," she murmured. "Beyond the door there is a small room, with a passage leading from it. It is the passage that is lit."

She looked around at them, her small face full of defiance, her dagger glinting in her hand. "I think we should enter," she said grimly. "Then whoever is laughing at us may wish they had kept silence." She put her shoulder against the door and pushed to open it further. Then she turned to Lief. "Are you coming?" she demanded.

Lief stepped forward. But at the same moment Prin bounded in front of him. "No!" she begged. "No, Lief! You at least must not!" Taken by surprise, Lief stumbled, lost his footing, and fell heavily.

He lay on the ground, dazed, staring up at the door. The grooved lines, tall on the pale stone, seemed to shimmer above him. Then — then, to his astonishment, he suddenly saw them for what they were.

Words. The lines were words. He blinked, hardly believing what he was seeing. But it was true. The letters had been stretched tall and narrowed so much that he had not realized they were any more than decoration. But looking at them from below, he could read what they said.

IF YOU WISH TO DIE.

"Lief, I am sorry . . ." Prin was bending over him anxiously.

Barda was staring at them, his hand on the stone. But Jasmine, shaking her head impatiently, was stepping through the door.

"Jasmine — " Lief spluttered, scrambling to his feet. "Do not go in. Jasmine! It is a trap!"

He leaped forward, catching Jasmine by the wrist just as, with a cry, she plunged into the pit that yawned beyond the door.

13 - Within

Jasmine swung helplessly, Lief's grip on her wrist the only thing that was saving her from crashing to the bottom of the trap into which she had stumbled.

The pit was deep, but still Lief could see a white glimmer at the bottom. His stomach turned over as he realized they were bones — the bones of other intruders, no doubt. The gnomes had probably been watching through peepholes in the rock as the companions tried to open the door. One had laughed aloud, believing that there were about to be three more victims of the deadly joke. Lief gritted his teeth in anger.

Then Barda was kneeling beside him, and together they were lifting Jasmine up, swinging her to safety.

"We must do the opposite of what the verse

says," said Lief. "We must pull the door, not push it, if we are to enter safely."

They pulled the door until it clicked shut. Then they unlocked it with the arrow once more, and pulled again. Sure enough, the huge piece of stone grated as easily outward as it had inward.

Barda picked up a few arrows and threw them into the darkness where the pit had been. They clanged on metal.

"It is as I thought," said Lief. "The pit is usually covered. It is only when the door is pushed inward that the cover slides away."

"A devilish device," growled Barda. "If you and I had not hesitated, Lief — "

"I *told* you the gnomes were clever," Prin broke in. "They are clever, hate strangers, and love cruel jokes. We must be very, very careful. If they are still watching, they know their trick has failed. They will try something else."

This time no one argued with her.

They entered the door, tapping the earth in front of them with their shields to check it for safety, listening for any sound of movement. But all was silence. Ahead was the long tunnel they had seen from the entrance.

Their faces ghostly in the light of the flickering torches, they began to creep along the tunnel. Only Jasmine and Prin could stand upright, and even they had to bend their heads. Soon the tunnel turned sharply, and almost at once turned again. Then they came to a place where it split into three. One passage led to the left, one led to the right, and one led straight ahead.

"Which way?" whispered Lief.

"There is no way of telling which path is safest," growled Barda. "But I think we should take the one that goes straight ahead. It has a higher ceiling than the others. If we take either of the other two, I will have to crawl."

They moved on. Still there was utter silence. They saw that just ahead the tunnel once again took a sharp right turn.

"Perhaps, after all, the gnomes think we are in the pit," said Jasmine in a low voice, as they moved around the corner into dimmer light.

"Perhaps," Barda answered grimly. "But I would not depend upon it. I think — "

He broke off and halted abruptly. There were some shadowy figures ahead, blocking their path. Barda and Lief raised their swords. An answering glint showed that their opponents were also armed, and by their shape carried shields also.

"Dread Gnomes, we come in peace," Barda called. "We ask only that you listen to what we have to say. We will put down our weapons if you also will disarm."

There was no answering call, and no movement except for the gleam of steel.

"We must not let them think we are afraid," Jasmine whispered, and slowly the companions began to move forward again. The figures moved also, coming to meet them, matching them stride for stride.

"Why do you not answer?" Barda called again. "Do you want to fight? If so, we are ready and willing." He quickened his pace. Lief and Jasmine strode after him. Shuffling behind them, trying to keep up, Prin gave a muffled whimper of fear.

In moments the figures were almost upon them, still shadowy, but looming large. They are much bigger than we expected. And there are four of them, Lief thought, tightening his grip on his sword.

Hand-to-hand combat. He had not expected this. But he was ready. He lifted his shield. One of his opponents did the same. And suddenly, suddenly Lief saw . . .

"Barda, it is a mirror! A mirror fixed to a wall!" he shouted. "This tunnel is a dead end!" A chill ran through his body as he heard a clicking sound behind him. He spun around, stumbling over Prin, trying to push past her, trying to get to the metal door that was sliding from the roof of the tunnel at her back.

But it was too late. By the time he reached it, the metal door was sealed shut. They were trapped. They were locked in an airless cell. A cell as escape-proof as a tomb.

✳

Hours later, they stood huddled together in thick darkness. They had put out the torch that was fixed to the wall. It was burning air they could not afford to lose.

"There must be a way out," Lief insisted. "There must!" He was swaying with weariness.

"The gnomes will come, surely," muttered Barda. "To jeer at us, if for no other reason. For what is the point of a joke no one laughs at? That will be our chance, for if they can get in, we can certainly get out."

Jasmine nodded. "We must be ready for them. We must have a plan. But when will they come? And how? If only we knew!"

"If we were at home, we could dream them," said a small voice behind them.

They all turned. They had almost forgotten about Prin. She crouched in a corner, her eyes enormous with fear, her paws clasped tightly in front of her.

"If we were at home with my tribe, we could drink the spring water, and remember the gnomes, and dream of them, wherever they are," she repeated softly. "We have seen them. Seen their faces . . ." Her voice trailed away and she began shivering all over. She heard Lief exclaim, and covered her face in shame.

"I am sorry," she whispered. "I have never been in walls before. I do not like it."

Filli chattered anxiously. Jasmine moved to

Prin's side and put her arm around her. "Do not be ashamed," she murmured. "I too fear being locked up. I fear it more than anything."

"You are very tired, little Kin," said Barda, with rough gentleness. "Lie down and sleep now. You can dream even without the spring water."

"But *with* it, how much more useful the dreams will be!" Lief burst out. As they all glanced at him curiously he grinned and held up his water bottle. "Do you not remember? I confess that I did not, until Prin reminded me just now. We have drunk from streams ever since we left the Kin. Our bottles are still full — with water from the Dreaming Spring!"

✳

Out of the mists of Lief's sleep, the dream slowly came into focus. Flickering light, dancing colors, a dull murmuring, the shuffling of many feet, clinking, chinking sounds . . . And one huge voice, terrifyingly loud, shockingly harsh, echoing, echoing . . . "MORE! GIVE ME MORE!"

Lief opened his eyes fully, stared, revolted, at the nightmare before him, and staggered back to press himself against the rocky wall. I am dreaming, he reminded himself wildly. Dreaming! I am here only in spirit. It cannot see me!

But still his heart thudded and his stomach churned. Whatever he had expected when he lay down to sleep, it was not this!

He had expected to see a cavern, though not so huge. The roof of this enormous space soared, surely, to the top of the Mountain.

He had expected to see treasure, though not in such great quantities. Great, glittering mounds of gold and jewels filled the cavern from wall to wall, rising into hills and dropping into valleys like the dunes of the Shifting Sands.

He had expected to see the gnomes he had seen on the mountaintop, though he had not thought to see them crawling, scuttling, shrinking, and afraid.

But the giant mass of lumpy, oozing flesh that squatted in the center of the cavern, its wicked eyes glazed with greed, its slimy clawed feet spread carelessly over tumbled gems and heaps of gold — this was something he had not expected. Not in his wildest imaginings.

It was a vast, toadlike beast. The hidden horror of Dread Mountain.

14 – Gellick

Gnomes crawled around the giant, collecting in great glass jars the slime that dripped from its skin like thick, oily drops of sweat. They all wore gloves and kept well away from the oozing drops, handling the jars with care.

The slime must be poisonous, thought Lief. Then, with a jolt, he realized that here must be the source of the venom that made the gnomes' arrows deadly.

As he watched, two other gnomes scuttled forward, bent under the weight of a huge golden bowl heaped high with what looked like black, glistening berries.

They knelt before the toad, heads bowed. Its long red tongue snaked out and curled in the black mass, scooping up a quarter of the contents of the bowl. As it lifted the feast to its huge mouth, scattering fragments carelessly over the gnomes and the treasure at its feet, Lief's stomach heaved. The food was not berries, but flies. Thousands — tens of thousands — of fat, dead flies.

In moments the bowl was empty. The toad gave a rasping growl of anger. "MORE! QUICKLY!" it roared.

The two kneeling gnomes cowered, glancing at each other fearfully. "Your pardon, great Gellick," faltered the one on the left, a wizened old man in a tattered brown jacket. "But — it may take some time to collect more from the breeding caves. The ready supplies are gone."

"WHAT? GONE? WHO IS RESPONSIBLE FOR THIS?" grated the toad.

The old gnome was trembling all over, but finally forced himself to speak. "It is just that you have eaten rather more today than usual, great Gellick," he quavered. "We were not prepared. We — "

His words were choked by a shriek as the toad spat at him without warning. He fell to the ground, writhing in agony. His terrified companion, wailing in grief and terror, dropped facedown beside him, clasping him in her arms as he died.

The other gnomes watched dumbly. On some faces Lief saw guilty thankfulness, because it was the old gnome who had been attacked, not them. On other faces there was sorrow and anger. But on most there was simply dull, blank hopelessness.

"Things on Dread Mountain are not as we thought," said Barda's voice behind him.

Startled, Lief swung around. Barda and Jasmine were standing near him. He could see them quite clearly, though they were shadowy and their outlines seemed to waver. Jasmine, for once without Filli and Kree, who had not drunk the dreaming water, was pale with disgust and anger.

"This is a vile thing," she muttered. "This Gellick rules the gnomes as the Wennbar ruled the Wenn in the Forests of Silence. But it is much worse. It kills not for food, but for spite alone."

"The gem we seek must be here," Barda said. "But how are we to find it? The cavern is piled high with precious stones."

Lief shook his head, amazed that he could have forgotten their quest, even for a moment. But forgotten it he had. The toad Gellick had absorbed all his attention.

Now he could feel that the Belt of Deltora had warmed against his skin. The fifth gem was here, in this cavern. But where?

"We will not be in a position to find the gem at all, if we do not get out of the prison they have us in!" Jasmine whispered fiercely.

"We must wait, and listen," Barda answered. "That is why we are here."

They watched as the body of the old gnome was dragged away by his sobbing companion. Slowly the other gnomes went back to their work of attending to the glass jars that collected the toad's slime. As each jar was filled, two gnomes carried it between them through a door near to where the companions were standing.

"Once we were a proud people," Lief heard one of these gnomes mutter disgustedly, as she passed. "Once we owned this treasure, and the Mountain was beautiful, fruitful and ours. Now we are slaves on a nest of thorns, farming flies for a toad."

"DID YOU SPEAK, GLA-THON?" The harsh voice filled the cavern.

The gnome who had spoken spun around hastily. "No. No, great Gellick," she lied. "Or, at least, if I did speak, it was only to say that the intruders — the intruders we told you about — are safely locked in the tomb-tunnel, and will not escape."

"THEY MUST DIE!"

"Oh, they will die, my lord," said another gnome, stepping forward and smoothing his red beard. "The simpler ones among us have been watching them, enjoying their feeble efforts to escape. But the sport has ended now for they have put out the light. By morning they will be dead through lack of air. Then we will drag them into the breeding caves, and the flies can have them."

He beamed, bowing low. "And soon you, great Gellick, will have the flies," he added. "It is a fine progress, is it not?"

The giant toad almost seemed to smile. "You are clever, Ri-Nan," it growled. "But not clever enough, it seems, to ensure that my food is brought to me on time, as was the bargain."

Its voice was low now, and husky. But somehow this was even more terrible than its loudest roar. Its eyes gleamed with malice. The red-bearded gnome backed away, the smile that still lingered on his lips stiffening into a snarl of fear.

"You deserve punishment, Ri-Nan," rasped Gellick softly. "But you are useful to me, so perhaps I will forgive you. Or perhaps I will not. I will think on it. In the meantime, take the rest of these miserable slaves to the breeding caves and work there with them for the rest of the night. Tomorrow there will be flies enough — or you will suffer for it."

Ri-Nan scuttled for the door, stumbling over the piles of treasure in his haste, beckoning to the other gnomes to follow him. In moments, the cavern was still.

Satisfied, the monster settled itself more comfortably and licked some stray flies from its lips. It half-closed its eyes and lowered its great head.

And it was then that Lief saw the dull green stone sunk into its brow and, with a thrill of horror, knew it for what it was.

The emerald. The symbol of honor. The fifth gem of the Belt of Deltora.

✳

The companions woke together in the heavy darkness of their prison. It was like waking from a nightmare, a nightmare they had all shared. And yet — they knew only too well that what they had seen was real.

"Did you discover anything of use?" they heard Prin ask eagerly, as she heard them stir.

Jasmine crawled to her feet. "One thing we learned is that before we put out the light the gnomes were watching us," she said. "But how? I am sure there is not a gap or hole anywhere in this accursed cell."

Feeling her way, she began examining the walls, the roof, and even the floor again, leaving it to Barda and Lief to tell Prin the rest of the story. They told it as gently as they could, but by the time they had finished the little Kin was again shivering with fear.

"Never have I heard of such a thing," she whispered. "My people know nothing of it. So this is why the gnome-rests and paths are so badly overgrown, and why the gnomes look so sickly pale. They are underground almost all the time, collecting this toad's poison for their arrows, and serving his needs."

"I think you are right," muttered Lief.

They heard Jasmine stamping her foot in anger. "I can find nothing!" she hissed. "Not the tiniest crack."

"If there *was* a crack, there would be air," said Lief drearily. "And there is no air."

"But they *watched* us!" Jasmine insisted. "It

102

sounded as though many watched at once, laughing at our foolish efforts to escape. That gnome Gla-Thon spoke of it as if it was as easy as staring through a window!"

Barda gave a muffled cry, and scrambled to his feet. "Why, perhaps it was!" he whispered.

"What do you mean?" Jasmine demanded. "There is no window here!"

"No window we can see," said Barda. He edged past Lief to put his fingers against the mirror.

"I once heard a traveller tell of a miracle he had seen: a glass that was a mirror on one side and a window on the other," he said. "I thought he was just making up tall tales to earn free drinks at the tavern. But perhaps I was unjust."

"There is only one way to find out," Lief said quietly.

"Quite so," Barda agreed. "And there is no time like the present. Draw your weapons and stand back."

He set one of the bark shields against the mirror, drew back his heavy boot, and kicked with all his strength. The mirror shattered, crashing out into a room beyond the cell. Dazzling light flooded through the gap — light, and air, and a smell so foul, so disgusting, that the companions choked as they stepped forward blindly, broken glass crunching under their feet.

"What is it?" coughed Jasmine, pressing her arm to her nose. "And what is that noise?"

But already their eyes were growing used to the light, and their stomachs churned as they saw what the room contained. Vast, netted cages lined the walls. And inside the cages were millions upon millions of flies, buzzing around stinking piles of rotting food.

"It is one of the breeding caves," said Lief. "Let us leave quickly. The gnomes may appear at any moment."

They hurried to the door and let themselves out into a dim tunnel. The sickening smell of decay still hung in the air. They could hear voices echoing from somewhere to their right. They turned to the left, but had not gone far when a door in front of them was thrown open and two gnomes came hurrying out, each carrying one end of a large wooden box.

The companions froze, then began backing away.

One of the gnomes, who Lief recognized as the red-bearded Ri-Nan, looked around, saw them, and yelled, dropping his corner of the box. His fellow stumbled and roared in anger as the box fell, hitting the stone floor sharply and splitting open. Dead flies spilled from it in a hideous, glistening stream.

"The intruders are escaping!" shrieked Ri-Nan. He threw back his head and gave the high, gobbling cry that the gnomes had used on the Mountainside when they were shooting at the Kin. Instantly the tunnel was filled with the echoing sound of pounding feet, coming from both directions.

"Back!" shouted Barda.

They ran for the door of the breeding cave they had just left. It was very near, but by the time they reached it both ends of the tunnel were filled with running gnomes, raising their bows, closing in on them.

Arrows had already begun to fly as Lief and Barda pushed Prin inside the cave and hurled themselves after her. They were safe, but Jasmine was not so lucky. As she leaped through the doorway she gave a shriek, and the gnomes howled in triumph.

She stumbled into the cave and fell back against the door, slamming it shut. Barda sprang to slide the bolt home. Lief caught Jasmine and dragged her aside as she slithered to the ground, pulling the quivering arrow from the palm of her hand.

15 – The Dread Gnomes

The wound was slight. The arrow had caught just under the skin. But Jasmine lay back, her eyes squeezed shut, gasping in agony as the poison surged through her body. Lief and Barda crouched over her, helpless and grief-stricken, as Filli moaned and Kree screeched.

"Why do you wait?" shrieked Prin. "Give her the potion! The magic potion that saved me!"

"There is none left," snapped Barda. "You had the last of it."

Prin shrank back, trembling.

Jasmine's eyes opened. "Do not listen to Barda. Do not blame yourself, Little One," she whispered through white lips. "You had to be saved. We owed it to your people. There is only one Prin."

"There is only one Jasmine," Barda muttered. His face was tight with grief.

The gnomes had reached the door. They were kicking and beating at it. Barda raised his head. "They will pay for this," he snarled. He stood up, his sword gleaming in his hand, his eyes burning.

"Do not — try to avenge me," Jasmine murmured. "Use your wits. Save yourselves. The quest — the Belt of Deltora — is more important than . . ."

She grimaced with pain. Her eyes closed. Filli whimpered piteously. Lief felt that his heart was breaking.

"The toad's venom is killing her!" sobbed Prin.

Venom.

With a cry, Lief tore the Belt of Deltora from his waist. Prin gasped through her tears and Barda looked down, frowning furiously. "Lief, what are you doing?" he demanded.

Lief paid no attention to either of them. He was pressing the medallion that held the dulled ruby against Jasmine's injured hand, folding her fingers over it, hoping against hope as words from *The Belt of Deltora* echoed in his mind.

✝ **The great ruby, symbol of happiness, red as blood . . . wards off evil spirits, and is an antidote to snake venom.**

If the ruby could combat snake venom, perhaps it would have an effect on Gellick's venom also. It was a slim chance. But it was all the chance they had.

He looked up, met Barda's eyes, and saw that

the big man at last understood what he was doing.

"She is still breathing. But we need time," Lief muttered. Barda nodded and turned again to face the door. Without a word, Prin took Jasmine's dagger and crept over to stand beside him. The big man glanced at her and tried to wave her away, but she shook her head and did not move.

The gnomes were battering the door with something heavy now, heaving and shouting in time. The door's bolt was rattling and the wood was beginning to splinter. It would not hold for much longer.

Barda stood grimly, sword in hand, waiting. Beside him, eyes wide and terrified, was Prin. She winced with every crash against the door, but stood her ground.

Jasmine lay deathly still, her fingers curled around the Belt. Lief bent his head and whispered in her ear. "Jasmine, fight the poison. Fight it!" he breathed. "The ruby is in your hand. The ruby is helping you."

Jasmine's face did not change. But Lief thought he saw the sun-browned fingers move, very slightly. She had heard him. He was sure of it.

There was another crash, and the sound of cracking wood. Kree cried a warning and flew to Barda. Prin squealed in terror. Lief turned and saw that the door was shuddering violently. Its hinges were bursting. The bolt had half fallen away. One more blow, or two . . .

Beside him, Jasmine gave a long, low sigh. He glanced down, and gasped in amazement. Red light was glowing between her curled fingers.

It was the ruby. The ruby, working its magic, showing its power.

Jasmine's eyes opened sleepily. Lief's heart leaped as he saw that they were clear, no longer filled with pain. But she was weak, terribly weak.

"Lief!" roared Barda. "They have broken through!"

Lief stood Jasmine's shield in front of her to give her some protection, and ran to the door. Through the gaping holes in the shuddering wood he could see grinning gnome faces and the glinting of axes.

Barda was flailing with his sword, slashing at the holes as gnome hands and feet crept forward. Prin was by his side, stabbing bravely with Jasmine's dagger. So far they had prevented entry. But it would not be long before the door gave way completely, falling inward. When that happened, the gnomes would rush over it like water over a collapsing dam. Then all would be lost.

"Prin!" Lief shouted. "Go to Jasmine! She is reviving, but slowly. Protect her, and Filli, if you can."

He took Prin's place as she hurried to do his bidding. Barda had never stopped beating the gnomes back, but his grim, sweating face was even more determined now that he knew Jasmine was still alive.

An angry voice shrilled from the other side of

the door. A voice Lief recognized. "You cannot win, you fools! Give in now and we will be merciful and kill you quickly. Keep us waiting here and we will make you pay! We will make you suffer!"

It was Gla-Thon, the worker who had complained about having to toil for Gellick. Lief licked his lips and shouted back.

"Are you afraid, Gla-Thon, that your master the toad will be angry if you dally with us here instead of collecting flies? Ah, there was once a time when gnomes were their own masters."

"And a time, I have heard, when the halls of Dread Mountain did not stink like garbage carts," Barda called, following Lief's lead. "And when their treasure was not covered in toad slime, but was the envy of all."

"Shut your mouths!" shrieked Gla-Thon in fury.

"The great toad has made us strong!" called another voice that Lief was sure belonged to the red-bearded Ri-Nan. "It came to us and offered to protect us from the Shadow Lord and his Guards. It offered to let us use its poison, on certain — conditions. These conditions were hard, but we were glad to accept them. Gellick's venom has made us powerful."

"Oh, yes," Lief jeered. "It helped you drive away the Kin, so that now your paths and gnome-rests are smothered by thorny Boolong trees in which Vraal can lie in wait. It enslaved you, so that now you toil day and night in Gellick's service, half starved and in fear of your lives. You have indeed made a wonderful bargain."

There was silence outside the door. Lief and Barda glanced at each other. Was it possible that they were winning this battle of words?

"We could help you rid yourselves of your tyrant," Lief called, crossing his fingers for luck. "Do you not want to be free again?"

There was another long silence.

"No weapon can kill Gellick." When it came at last, Gla-Thon's voice was dull with despair. "Gellick's hide is too thick for swords and arrows to pierce. Even axes have no effect. Many have paid with their lives for daring to try to win our freedom."

"No one can survive Gellick's venom," called another, older voice. "I, Fa-Glin, leader of the Dread Gnomes, tell you this. You saw yourself what happened to your companion — through just a tiny arrow wound in her hand."

"What happened to me?" The voice rang out, strong and laughing.

As a stunned silence fell outside the door, Lief and Barda spun around. Jasmine was standing behind them, leaning on Prin's shoulder. She looked pale and weak, but she grinned at them and wordlessly held out the Belt of Deltora. Lief took it, and quickly fastened it around his waist, covering it with his shirt once more.

"The venom did not harm me, Fa-Glin!" Jasmine

shouted. "Our magic is too strong. The toad cannot kill us, but we have weapons powerful enough to kill it."

She paused, swaying. Then she made a great effort, raised her head, and called again, her voice as confident as before. "Do you want our help? If so, lay down your weapons, send in three members of your party, and we will talk."

✳

The meeting between Barda, Lief, Jasmine, and the three representatives of the gnomes, Gla-Thon, Ri-Nan, and Fa-Glin, lasted for well over an hour. While it was taking place, Prin, Kree, and Filli watched silently from a corner of the breeding cave. None of them trusted the gnomes, and the fact that the white-bearded Fa-Glin wore a fringed jacket that was plainly made from Kin skin did little to change their minds.

Discussion was difficult and angry at first. But, as Lief had suspected, in her heart Gla-Thon was determined not to let the chance of defeating Gellick pass by. Fa-Glin, astounded by Jasmine's magical recovery, was on her side. And at last even Ri-Nan gave in and a decision was reached. With the gnomes' help, the visitors would kill Gellick. In return they would receive their freedom, and the dull green stone embedded in the toad's forehead.

"It seems a poor reward," murmured old Fa-Glin, regarding them with suspicion. "And how do you know it is there, may I ask? The stone appeared in Gellick's brow only a little more than sixteen years ago."

"We have ways of knowing such things," said Jasmine quickly. "Have you not seen for yourselves how strong our magic is?"

"I have heard tell that toad-stones can weave powerful spells," Gla-Thon put in. "And this one is very large." She turned to the companions. "No doubt that is why you want it?"

Lief, Barda, and Jasmine nodded, but they could see that Fa-Glin was not convinced. Plainly he was still not sure that they were to be trusted.

"Gellick will be sleeping now," Ri-Nan said. "Entering the treasure cavern at this time is forbidden. If Gellick wakes . . ."

"The toad will not wake," Barda said firmly. "And if it does, we are the ones who will suffer. We will enter the cavern alone. All we ask is that you show us the way."

Old Fa-Glin's eyes narrowed. "Enter the treasure cavern alone? So you can pick and choose whatever you wish to steal? Oh, no, there will be none of that."

"In any case," Gla-Thon put in, as Lief bit back the angry reply that trembled on his lips, "we might as well be with you. If the plan goes wrong we will pay as dearly as you in the end, for Gellick will blame us for letting you escape."

Lief glanced at Ri-Nan. The red-bearded gnome said nothing, but his eyes, under the bushy eyebrows, were wary and hard as stones.

Fa-Glin folded his arms. "Very well," he said. "It is agreed. The six of us will go together to the cavern, and there it will be Gellick's death, or our own." He turned and looked around at the fly cages, his wrinkled face a mask of shame and disgust. "If we succeed, we can rid our halls of this filth," he said. "If we fail — at least I will never have to see it again. I, for one, am happy to take the risk."

16 - Do or Die

Shortly afterwards Lief, Barda, and Jasmine were following the three gnomes as they threaded their way through tunnel after tunnel, growing ever closer to the center of the Mountain. They had made Prin stay behind with Kree and Filli, with instructions that she was to do all she could to escape with the others should they not return.

They had left their packs behind too and their shields. All they now carried were their basic needs: their weapons, their water bottles — and all their remaining blisters.

They planned to use the blisters to kill Gellick. None of them shrank from the idea of attacking the monster in its sleep. It deserved no fair play from them. Their only doubt was whether they could creep close enough to it to make their aim true, without causing it to wake.

The gnomes began to move more slowly and quietly, and soon the huge entrance to the cavern came into view. Even from a distance a rainbow shimmer could be seen beyond the door, as the cavern's torches cast flickering light on the treasure trove heaped below.

Without making a sound, they stole to the entrance and peeped in. The monster was still squatting in the center of the mounded jewels and gold, in exactly the same position as when Lief, Barda, and Jasmine had seen it in their dream. Its eyes were closed. Only a slow pulse in its throat and the slow runnels of slime oozing from its skin showed that it was not a huge and hideous statue, the creation of some twisted soul who worshipped ugliness and evil.

The three companions moved forward, and this time it was the gnomes who followed, keeping well back. Slowly they climbed the mound of treasure, watching their feet, their minds focused totally on the need for silence as gold and jewels shifted under their boots like pebbles.

They crept forward, one careful step at a time. Soon they would be close enough. Gellick had not moved. Lief drew a long breath and tightened his grip on the blister he had ready in his hand. If ever I have thrown straight, hard, and true, I must do so now, he told himself.

One more step, another . . .

"Great Gellick! Beware!" The scream shattered

the silence. Lief spun around. The red-bearded Ri-Nan was rushing past him, scrabbling over the treasure, waving his arms. "I have come to warn you, great Gellick!" he screeched. "Treachery!"

The toad's eyes opened.

"Now!" Barda roared. Lief threw the blister as hard and fast as he could. It was the throw of his life. He yelled in triumph as the blister hit the monster full in the throat while in the same instant Barda's blister, and Jasmine's, burst on its chest. Lief threw his second blister, shouting as he saw it burst in the same place as before, waiting for Gellick to tremble and fall.

But nothing happened. The creature's eyes did not flicker. Lazily, its tongue snaked out and licked at the poison running, gleaming, down its chest. Its great mouth stretched wide in a mocking grin.

"Who are these foolish creatures who attack me with my own venom?" it rasped.

Thunderstruck, Lief, Barda, and Jasmine stumbled back, turning to Gla-Thon and Fa-Glin, who stood frozen in horror behind them.

"But — the gnomes collect Gellick's slime for themselves!" cried Jasmine. "How could it be in the blisters? How could — "

"We keep only a little," mumbled Gla-Thon, her lips stiff with fear. "The rest must be taken, at each full moon, to the bottom of the Mountain and left by the roadside. It was part of the bargain. We did not know — "

"RI-NAN," Gellick roared. "ANSWER ME! WHO ARE THEY?"

"They are the intruders, great Gellick!" gabbled Ri-Nan. He pointed at Gla-Thon and Fa-Glin. "And there are the traitors who set them free, and helped them find you. Kill them! I, your faithful servant, can make the gnomes work harder than that doddering fool Fa-Glin ever could. I should be leader. I, Ri-Nan, deserve your — "

He broke off as Gellick's awful eyes turned on him.

"Down, while it is not looking!" muttered Barda. "Hide under . . ."

"YOU *DESERVE*, RI-NAN?" roared the monster. "YOU DARE TO ORDER *ME*? *THIS* IS WHAT YOU DESERVE, WORM!"

It spat and Ri-Nan collapsed, screaming, rolling over and over, kicking and writhing among the gold. The toad's tongue flicked in satisfaction. Then it turned, slowly . . .

"Ah," it hissed, as it saw that the drifts of treasure now glittered empty in the flickering light. "Now you hide from me, do you, worms? You burrow under my trinkets, trembling at my rage? That is as it should be."

It lifted a huge foot, stamping with a sound like thunder, and its voice rose to a deafening roar. "I AM THE GREAT GELLICK! THE SHADOW LORD HIM-

SELF RESPECTS ME. MY VENOM ALONE DEFEATS HIS ENEMIES!"

The hideous bellow echoed around the cavern. Hidden below a glittering mass of coins and gems, scarcely able to breathe, Lief listened in terror. He knew his companions were somewhere near, but he did not dare move or speak as Gellick's voice roared on.

"HE GAVE ME THIS MOUNTAIN, AND A RACE OF SLAVES TO SERVE ME. HE KNOWS I WILL NOT FAIL HIM. HE TRUSTS ME TO KILL YOU, WORMS! HE TRUSTS ME TO GUARD THE STONE I WEAR ON MY BROW. OTHERS MAY HAVE FAILED HIM. BUT NOT I!"

Lief's thoughts were racing. The beast had been expecting them. It knew they had come for the emerald. The moment they raised their heads, the moment they moved to escape or attack, it would kill them.

Now it had fallen silent. It was waiting, watching, no doubt for any sign of movement. Long moments passed. At last it spoke again, its voice rasping, sneering, and low.

"I know where you are. I have only to wait, worms, till at last you show yourselves. But I choose not to wait. I choose instead to crush you where you lie."

There was a tumbling, clinking sound as gold and jewels were pushed aside. The toad was moving, crawling towards them, heaving its great bulk along on its vast, clawed feet. Nearer. Nearer . . .

"It will please me to feel you beneath my weight, and hear your screams, worms," it hissed. "It will please me to see what is left of your bodies dragged away at last, to feed the flies."

Lief lay very still. His sword was in his hand. He realized, almost with surprise, that he felt very calm. He had already decided that he would wait until the last moment, then spring up and try to pierce the beast's belly, whatever the gnomes had said. It would mean his death, but his death was coming in any case, one way or another.

The monster was very close now. So close that through the gaps in the jewels above his head Lief could see its shadow. The Belt of Deltora was burning at his waist. The Belt could feel the emerald — the emerald that would never shine again, but would remain dulled by the toad's evil.

Was it time yet to scramble from hiding, to make his last, hopeless gesture of defiance? No. A moment more. But no longer than that. Lief thought that Jasmine and Barda were somewhere behind him, with the two gnomes. But he could not be sure. His greatest fear now was that he would hear their anguished cries before he himself could escape into death. That he could not face.

His thoughts drifted to Kree, Filli, and Prin, waiting near the breeding cave. He hoped that the gnomes would let them go. That they would escape from the Mountain safely. That, somehow, Kree and Filli could make their way back to the Forests of Silence and Prin would return to the Kin. Prin, who looked so like the companion of his earliest childhood come to life.

He smiled slightly as he remembered the first time he had seen her, drinking from the Dreaming Spring.

Drink, gentle stranger, and welcome. All of evil will beware.

It was as though Lief had been struck by lightning. For a split second everything seemed to stand still. Then he moved his hand from his sword hilt to his belt.

The coins and jewels above him were swept away by a huge, clawed foot.

"I SEE YOU, WORM!"

The monster was above him, its great head bending low, its mouth open in a leer of triumph. But already Lief had pulled the water bottle free, and unscrewed its cap. And before the toad could jeer again, he was hurling the bottle, overflowing with water from the Dreaming Spring, straight into the grinning, open mouth, to the back of the throat.

He struggled to his knees as Gellick gulped. The giant toad hissed.

"YOU —" it choked. Then it jerked violently and its eyes rolled back in its head. It tried to move, but already its feet were fixed to the treasure hill by thick, snaking roots. It screamed. It screamed as its swollen body pulsed and changed. It screamed as its vast, spiny neck began to stretch.

Then there were some long, terrifying moments when Lief wanted to turn away, but could not. Moments when he heard Jasmine and Barda beside him, but could do no more than clasp their hands. Moments when the whole cavern seemed to flash and darken, when he thought that the monstrous, writhing thing before him would never cease its struggles.

Then all was still, and where Gellick had crouched there was a vast tree with a straight, tall trunk and three branches bearing clusters of pale-colored leaves. The tree's topmost branches brushed the soaring roof of the treasure cavern. And as Lief looked up, something fell from its tip, straight into his hand.

It was the emerald. Dull no longer, but deep, sparkling green.

Fa-Glin and Gla-Thon were watching, goggle-eyed. But Lief did not hesitate. The Belt of Deltora gleamed as he put its fifth stone in place.

17 - Farewell

Great was the rejoicing in the halls of the Dread Gnomes that day. The treasure cavern seethed with gnomes gazing in awe at the tree that now rose in its center. The locked doors of the food stores were opened and a great feast was enjoyed by all. Thanks and praise were heaped on the companions' heads as the story of Gellick's defeat was told and retold.

"I feared the worst," said Fa-Glin to a crowd of listeners, for the dozenth time. "I thought we were lost. Then Lief of Del wrought his great magic, and in an instant all was changed."

And for the dozenth time the crowd sighed in awe, and Lief felt uncomfortable. Fa-Glin's tale made it sound as though he had meant all along to use the Dreaming Water, and had simply waited until the time was right. In fact, of course, it was the impulse of a moment, an idea that sprang into his mind when all seemed lost.

But he said nothing aloud. He could see the wisdom of Barda's whispered advice: "It will do us no harm for the Dread Gnomes to think we can perform wonders. They are a warlike and suspicious people. There will come a time when we will need their loyalty and their trust, when we will want them to listen to our advice."

In fact that time came sooner than they expected. The feast was still in progress when there was a high, gobbling cry from somewhere near. Then there was the sound of running feet.

"Kin!" a voice shouted. "Pen-Fel and Za-Van have sighted Kin from the spyholes to the south. There are many, many. The sky is black with them!"

In an instant, food and drink were forgotten, bows and arrows were being snatched up, and gnomes were running for the door.

"No!" Lief, Barda, Jasmine, and Prin shouted at the tops of their voices. Their voices echoed around the feasting hall.

And the gnomes stopped.

"Have you not learned better than this?" demanded Lief, as Prin clung to him in terror. "Do you not realize that the Kin should be your partners on this Mountain? Do you want the Boolong trees to continue to multiply till even the streams are choked by thorns? If I am right, the Kin are coming to rescue their young one. You should rejoice, and beg them to stay! You should welcome them with open arms, not seek to kill them!"

There was a moment's silence, then Fa-Glin nodded. "Our friend is right," he said. Regretfully he smoothed the old Kin skin jacket he wore, then he took it off and threw it at his feet.

"It is a pity. But our weavers can make fine garments enough," he murmured. Then once again he raised his voice. "Lay down your weapons, gnomes. We will go out and greet the Kin in friendship. We will welcome them home."

✳

At sunrise two days later, a strange group walked down the gnomes' pathway to the bottom of the Mountain. Prin walked with Lief, Jasmine, and Barda. Ailsa, Merin, and Bruna came next. Fa-Glin and Gla-Thon brought up the rear.

They spoke little as they walked, for more than one heart was heavy at the thought of the parting to come. But when they reached the road at the Mountain's base, where a bridge spanned the stream, they turned to one another.

"We thank you and will think of you every day," Ailsa murmured, bending and touching each of the travellers on the forehead. "Because of you we are home, and Little — I mean, Prin — is with us once more."

Merin smiled as she and Bruna farewelled the

companions in their turn. "As she has told us many times, Prin has grown too tall and strong in these last days to be called Little One anymore. Besides, now that we are here again, there will be more young, and she will no longer be the smallest among us."

As she stepped back, Fa-Glin stepped forward. "The Dread Gnomes also thank you," he said gruffly, bowing low. He held out his hand and Gla-Thon passed him a small carved box of Boolong tree bark. This Fa-Glin gave to Lief.

Lief opened the box. Inside was a golden arrowhead. "We owe you a great debt," said Fa-Glin. "If ever you need us, we are yours to the death. And this is a token of our oath."

"Thank you," said Lief, and bowed in his turn. "And you will follow the plan . . . ?"

"Indeed we will." Fa-Glin's teeth gleamed through his white beard as he grinned. "Next full moon, and every full moon from now on, the poison jars will be at this spot as usual. But their contents will not be the same, though the liquid will look identical. Stream water mixed with Boolong sap, I fancy, will do the trick. We and the Kin together will make the brew. It has been decided."

"And our last supplies of Gellick's venom will be kept safe," added Gla-Thon. "So that when at last our Enemy realizes what we are doing, and comes for us, we will be ready. Then, and only then, will our arrows be tipped with poison once more."

"It is our hope — " Barda hesitated, then went on carefully. "It is our hope that your Mountain will not be invaded. Before long there may come a time when the Enemy will have other concerns."

The Kin glanced at one another, confused. But Fa-Glin and Gla-Thon nodded, their eyes gleaming. They had sworn never to speak of the stone that had fallen into Lief's hand, or of what he had done with it. They had not asked for an explanation of the glittering, gem-studded Belt into which the emerald had fitted, or the two empty spaces that still glared blankly along the Belt's length. But perhaps they did not need to ask. Perhaps they knew, or guessed, the truth, for the Dread Gnomes were an old race, with long, long memories.

Lief felt Prin's gentle touch on his shoulder. "Where are you going now, Lief?" he heard her ask.

Lief looked across the bridge to where the stream continued through rustling trees, and on to where the first rays of the sun glinted on broader water: the distant river that would take them to the wide sea and the forbidden place that was their next goal.

"I must not tell you, Prin," he said softly. "But it is a long way from here."

"And why are you going? And why so soon?" she persisted, for the moment, in her distress, becoming again that more childish Prin he remembered from the time when they first met.

"Because I must," Lief said. "And because there

is no time to waste. We must finish our journey as quickly as we can, now. There are people at home who are — waiting."

And as he turned to meet Prin's eyes, to say the hardest farewell of all, he prayed that the wait would not be too long.